Clint ha... McBeth, but that wasn't going to happen. As one gunman turned on him, he drew and fired one shot. Clint hit the man dead center, drove him back off the dock and into the water with a splash. Then Clint turned his attention to the other three men, who had charged at their target, and he could tell by the way they held their knives that they were not experienced knife fighters.

McBeth dropped to the ground and managed to trip up two of the men. They went sprawling. McBeth disarmed the third man, then deposited him into the water. McBeth turned as one of the other men was getting up. They faced each other, each holding a knife. Then the sailor—not liking the new one-to-one odds—jumped back and ran away.

Clint approached McBeth. "You need one of them to tell you who hired them?" Clint asked.

"No," McBeth said, picking up his bag. "It was the captain of this ship. He was a friend of mine."

"Was?"

"Well, he tried to have me killed," McBeth said. "I think the friendship is over . . ."

# DON'T MISS THESE
# ALL-ACTION WESTERN SERIES
# FROM THE BERKLEY PUBLISHING GROUP

### THE GUNSMITH by J. R. Roberts
Clint Adams was a legend among lawmen, outlaws, and ladies. They called him . . . the Gunsmith.

### LONGARM by Tabor Evans
The popular long-running series about Deputy U.S. Marshal Custis Long—his life, his loves, his fight for justice.

### SLOCUM by Jake Logan
Today's longest-running action Western. John Slocum rides a deadly trail of hot blood and cold steel.

### BUSHWHACKERS by B. J. Lanagan
An action-packed series by the creators of Longarm! The rousing adventures of the most brutal gang of cutthroats ever assembled—Quantrill's Raiders.

### DIAMONDBACK by Guy Brewer
Dex Yancey is Diamondback, a Southern gentleman turned con man when his brother cheats him out of the family fortune. Ladies love him. Gamblers hate him. But nobody pulls one over on Dex . . .

### WILDGUN by Jack Hanson
The blazing adventures of mountain man Will Barlow—from the creators of Longarm!

### TEXAS TRACKER by Tom Calhoun
J.T. Law: the most relentless—and dangerous—manhunter in all Texas. Where sheriffs and posses fail, he's the best man to bring in the most vicious outlaws—for a price.

# THE GUNSMITH

### 329

## THE DUBLIN DETECTIVE

## J. R. ROBERTS

**J**

JOVE BOOKS, NEW YORK

**THE BERKLEY PUBLISHING GROUP**
**Published by the Penguin Group**
**Penguin Group (USA) Inc.**
**375 Hudson Street, New York, New York 10014, USA**
Penguin Group (Canada), 90 Eglinton Avenue East, Suite 700, Toronto, Ontario M4P 2Y3, Canada
(a division of Pearson Penguin Canada Inc.)
Penguin Books Ltd., 80 Strand, London WC2R 0RL, England
Penguin Group Ireland, 25 St. Stephen's Green, Dublin 2, Ireland (a division of Penguin Books Ltd.)
Penguin Group (Australia), 250 Camberwell Road, Camberwell, Victoria 3124, Australia
(a division of Pearson Australia Group Pty. Ltd.)
Penguin Books India Pvt. Ltd., 11 Community Centre, Panchsheel Park, New Delhi—110 017, India
Penguin Group (NZ), 67 Apollo Drive, Rosedale, North Shore 0632, New Zealand
(a division of Pearson New Zealand Ltd.)
Penguin Books (South Africa) (Pty.) Ltd., 24 Sturdee Avenue, Rosebank, Johannesburg 2196,
South Africa

Penguin Books Ltd., Registered Offices: 80 Strand, London WC2R 0RL, England

THE DUBLIN DETECTIVE

A Jove Book / published by arrangement with the author

PRINTING HISTORY
Jove edition / May 2009

ISBN: 978-0-515-14628-8

JOVE®
Jove Books are published by The Berkley Publishing Group,
a division of Penguin Group (USA) Inc.,
375 Hudson Street, New York, New York 10014.
JOVE® is a registered trademark of Penguin Group (USA) Inc.
The "J" design is a trademark of Penguin Group (USA) Inc.

PRINTED IN THE UNITED STATES OF AMERICA

10   9   8   7   6   5   4   3   2   1

# ONE

James McBeth stared down at the docks from the deck of the *Dublin Queen*. He stretched, trying to dispel the kink in his lower back.

"What'dja expect," asked Captain Angus O'Callaghan. "I tol' ya we wasn't a passenger ship."

McBeth looked at his friend and said, "I got just what I expected, you old pirate."

He'd had to find himself a corner in the ship's hold to sleep in. It was cramped and damp, and if a kink in his back was the worst he'd have to deal with, he'd take it. He could have gotten pneumonia, scurvy or worse.

"Ya better get you off this ship if you wan'ta get a room," the captain said. "My men already know all the good places."

"After the hold of your ship, anything will suffice," McBeth said.

"*Suffice*," O'Callaghan said. "If I was you, boyo, I'd watch meself wit' them ten-dollar words ya like ta use. The Barbary Coast ain't the place for them."

"I'll keep it in mind, Angus."

They continued to watch as most of the crew disembarked.

"He's got a week's head start on you, McBeth," O'Callaghan said. "What makes you think you can find him . . . out there?"

"It's what I do, Angus," McBeth said. "I'm a hunter of men, remember?"

"In our country, yes," the ship captain said. "But here?"

McBeth looked at O'Callaghan.

"Anywhere, Angus," he said. "It doesn't matter where. It's who I am."

"All right," O'Callaghan said. "We'll be here for four days, if you want to head back."

"I'm good," McBeth said with a grin, "but I don't think I'll find him that quickly."

"What if he's left San Francisco?"

"I already expect that he's left San Francisco," McBeth said. "He knows I'm after him. He'll go east, into this country's wilderness."

"Not so much of a wilderness anymore, as I hear," O'Callaghan said.

"Perhaps not."

"You'll have to be armed."

McBeth pulled aside his jacket to show the gun in his belt. It was German.

"You'll need better than that."

"I will get it," McBeth said.

"Well, then, I guess all that is left is for me to wish you luck, my friend."

McBeth turned and accepted O'Callaghan's hand.

"Thanks for the ride."

"Be careful."

"That's not how I do what I do," McBeth said, "but thanks for the sentiment."

McBeth walked to the gangplank, waited his turn to walk down. He hefted the bag on his back, which held only meager belongings. He would have to outfit himself, and he had planned in advance so that he had American money on him.

When he reached the dock he turned and looked up at O'Callaghan, who lifted his arm and waved. For McBeth, it was a friend waving good-bye to another friend—and perhaps it was, but it was not the kind of good-bye McBeth thought it was.

McBeth turned back around and looked ahead on the gangplank just in time to see the four men disembarking in front of him suddenly pivot and begin to rush him.

From the deck of the ship Captain Angus O'Callaghan watched the four men converge on McBeth. It hadn't been an easy thing for him to do, but he'd been paid a lot of money to make it look like McBeth had been killed on American soil during a robbery. That was why he hadn't had him killed on his ship.

O'Callaghan had known McBeth for a long time, so he couldn't watch the attack. He turned and walked away.

McBeth dropped the bag from his back. The four men faced him, one pointing a gun at the Irishman.

"Drop yer weapon," the gunman said.

The other three had knives. It was plain to McBeth that was the way they intended to kill him. They didn't want to shoot him, they wanted to make it look like he'd been knifed the minute he stepped off the boat.

"If I drop my gun, you'll kill me," McBeth replied.

"If you don't, we'll kill ye anyway," the man holding the gun said. "If ye drop yer gun, ye've got a fightin' chance at least."

McBeth thought about that for all of a second, and it actually made sense. If he tried to draw his gun, he might get one of them, but they'd surely kill him. If he dropped the weapon, they'd come at him with their knives. At least that way he'd have that fighting chance.

"Okay," he said.

"Take it out with two fingers," the man said. "Carefully now."

McBeth showed his two fingers, pulled his jacket aside, and drew the gun out that way, then dropped it to the ground.

"Kick it into the water."

Damn! He'd been hoping he could just kick it away and then maybe be able to pick it up during the fight. Once it was in the water, it was lost to him for good.

"Go on, boyo," the man said. "Kick it."

McBeth had no choice. He kicked the gun. It skittered across the dock and splashed into the water.

The man with the gun stepped back and said, "All right, lads. Do it."

More bad news. McBeth had been hoping the man would put his gun away and draw a knife. Instead, he was going to stand back and watch the other three kill him. And if, somehow, McBeth gained the upper hand, the gunman would probably just shoot him after all.

It looked bad for McBeth either way.

# TWO

The three sailors came at him, and he could tell from the way they held their knives that's what they were—sailors, not killers. They'd taken this job for the money, because there were four of them. If not for the man with the gun, McBeth felt he actually would have a fighting chance against them. If he could work his way around to the man with the gun, he wouldn't even have to take it from him, he'd just have to knock it away.

But at the moment the other three were between him and the gunman, fanned out, holding their knives like sailors, not like knife fighters.

He was going to have to get a knife away from one of them and risk a throw at the gunman.

"All right, then, lads," he said, "you heard the man— come and get me."

"Oh, we'll get ya, all right," one of them said. "That's what we're gettin' paid ta do."

"Enough talk," the man with the gun said. "Just do it so we can get on wit' our leave."

If the three men charged him all at once, he wasn't going to have a chance, whether they were experienced fighters or not. They'd take him down by sheer numbers.

He was good, but in this case, he was as good as dead.

"Hold it!"

Everybody looked toward the voice—McBeth, the man with the gun, and the three amateur knife fighters.

"Wha—" one of the sailors said.

There was a man standing there, his hands clasped in front of him. He was wearing a gun and looking very calm.

"Am I interrupting something?"

"A murder, I think," McBeth said.

"This ain't none of your business," the man with the gun said.

"Well, I was supposed to meet somebody down here on the dock," the stranger said, "but it looks like they haven't shown up. So I guess I don't have any business of my own." He shrugged. "I might as well get involved in yours."

"I don't mind," McBeth said.

"What have these men got against you, friend?" the stranger asked.

"Nothin' that I know of," McBeth said. "They are just bein' paid to kill me."

"By whom?"

"A friend of mine."

The man frowned.

"You got weird friends."

"Hey!" the gunman said. "Look, boyo, you should be on your way."

"Wait, I'm getting it," the stranger said. "You're all Irish, right? Just got off a boat from Dublin?"

"Galway," McBeth said. "But for all I know, they might be Dubliners."

The three men with the knives looked confused. McBeth thought that if the stranger kept the gunman busy, he'd be able to surprise the other three, maybe shove a couple of them into the water before they knew what was happening, leaving him with only one attacker to handle.

"Four against one," the stranger said. "Those aren't very fair odds. Why don't we start with you putting the gun down?"

"What?"

"Put it down," the man said. "Then you and me, we can watch your boys take on . . . what's your name?"

"McBeth."

"We can watch them take on Mr. McBeth," the man said. "Frankly, I'm willing to bet on him. Your boys don't look very smart."

"What?" The gunman was confused as well.

"Put it down."

The man flexed his fingers around the butt of the gun.

"Don't get nervous," the stranger told him. "You fire that thing, even by accident, and I'm going to have to kill you."

"I-I got my gun in my hand, friend."

"That doesn't matter to me . . . friend. You're in America now. We're all fast-draw artists. Haven't you read any of the books?"

"You mean, like Wild Bill Hickok?" McBeth asked.

"Exactly like Wild Bill Hickok."

McBeth looked at the gunman.

"If I were you, lad, I'd put it down."

The gunman risked a look at his ship, but there was nobody watching from the deck. He licked his lips while the three men with knives turned to look at him.

"Kill him!" he told them as he turned his gun toward the stranger.

# THREE

Clint had been hoping to talk the sailors out of killing the other man, but obviously that wasn't going to happen. As the gunman turned on him, he drew and fired one shot. He hit the man dead center, drove him back off the dock and into the water with a splash.

Clint turned his attention to the other three men, who had charged at their target. He could tell by the way they held their knives that they were not experienced knife fighters.

He watched as McBeth dropped to the ground and managed to trip up two of the men. They went sprawling as McBeth got back to his feet and disarmed the third man, then deposited him into the water.

McBeth turned as one of the other men was getting up. They faced each other, each holding a knife. Then the sailor—not liking the new one-to-one odds—jumped back and ran away.

Clint ejected the spent shell from his gun, replaced it with a live one, then holstered the gun and walked over to where McBeth was leaning over the felled body of the last attacker on the gangplank.

When Clint reached him, McBeth straightened up.

"He fell on his knife."

Clint looked toward the water. The man he'd shot was floating facedown. The other man who had fallen into the water was gone. He had probably crawled out farther down the block and run away.

"You need one of them to tell you who hired them?" Clint asked.

"No," McBeth said picking up his bag. "It was the captain of this ship."

"You want to go aboard and get him?" Clint asked. "I'll back your play."

"No," McBeth said, "As I told you, he was a friend of mine."

"Was?"

"Well, he tried to have me killed," McBeth said. "I think the friendship is over."

"But you're going to let him go?"

"Aye, I am."

"How come?"

"He was paid to hire it done," McBeth said. "Make it look like a robbery."

"And doesn't that upset you?"

"It tells me I'm on the right trail."

"Trail?"

"I'm looking for a man," McBeth said. "A killer. He came to this country to escape me."

"Okay."

"He probably offered the captain more money than he's ever seen," McBeth went on. "I can't blame him for taking it."

"That's very understanding of you."

"There's just no point in going back aboard that ship," McBeth said. "I've got work to do."

"Work?"

"I'm a Garda."

Clint frowned.

"I'm sorry," McBeth said. "Here you would say I'm a policeman—or lawman."

"Ah, I see."

"Do you know of a hotel near here?" McBeth asked.

"I know of a lot," Clint said, "but they're not fit for any kind of extended stay."

"Oh, I only need a room for one night," McBeth said, "perhaps two."

"What about a drink? And a meal?"

"That would be brilliant."

"Come on," Clint said. "I know someplace you can get all three."

# FOUR

Clint walked McBeth away from the Barbary Coast, closer to Portsmouth Square. They stopped in front of the Black Diamond Hotel.

"I can't afford this, boyo," McBeth said,

"That's okay," Clint said. "I know the owner, and I have a room here. They have great steaks. When's the last time you had a steak?"

McBeth laughed and said, "A long time."

"Come on," Clint said, "it's on me."

"On you?"

"I mean that I'll pay," Clint said. "For the dinner. And I'll get you a good price on a room. Come on. We'll talk over a couple of thick steaks."

McBeth shrugged and they went inside.

The Black Diamond was a smaller version of the grand hotels and gambling halls on the square. It catered to the crowd that existed between the plushness of Portsmouth Square and the squalor of the Barbary Coast.

Clint had been staying at the Black Diamond for four days, taking most of his meals there. He usually got the same waiter, Billy, and he was glad to see the young man again.

"Billy," he said, "my new friend needs a thick steak, and I'll take one, too."

"Sure thing, Mr. Adams. He just get to town?"

"Just got off the boat, Billy," Clint said. "And we'll take a couple of cold beers to go with it."

"Comin' up."

"Adams?" McBeth asked. "That's your name?"

"Clint Adams, yeah," Clint said.

"And what are you doing in San Francisco?" McBeth asked. "You said on the dock you were lookin' for some-one. Who was it?"

"Just somebody who was supposed to have some infor-mation for me."

"I see."

"Are you wearing a gun?" Clint asked. "I think I can see a rig under your coat."

"Aye, I wear one," McBeth said, "but that feller with the gun got the drop on me, so now I have a holster and no weapon. It's in the water." He held his coat open to show the empty holster.

"That won't be a problem to replace," Clint said, "unless it was a favorite of yours."

"Don't have favorite guns, Mr. Adams," McBeth said. "It's just a tool to me."

"Probably a good way to think of them," Clint said.

Billy came back with two cold beers and set them down on the table.

"Steaks are comin' up, gents."

"Good, Billy, good," Clint said.

McBeth wasted no time picking up the beer and drink-ing half of it down.

"Oh, aye," he said, setting it down, "I needed that, I did."

Clint drank some of his and also set the mug down.

"You want to tell me about this fellow you're hunting?" Clint asked. "Maybe I can help."

"How long have you been here?" McBeth asked.

"About four days."

"The man I'm after probably got here about a week ago."

"Maybe he stayed in San Francisco long enough for me to spot him."

"His name is Jamie Dolan."

"Jamie?"

"It's an Irish name."

"What's he look like?"

"Big, ugly, mid-thirties," McBeth said. "Likes to kill with his hands."

"Who?" Clint asked.

"What do you mean?"

"I mean who does he like to kill?" Clint asked.

"Oh, women and children."

"Children?"

"Young girls mostly."

Clint shook his head.

"I can't understand men like that," he said, "and I've known a lot of them."

"This one's an animal."

"Why did he come to this country?"

"He knows I'm following him," McBeth said. "Wherever he goes, he knows I'll follow."

"But why come here?"

"Because this gets me away from the other Garda—from my colleagues. Here it's just him an' me."

"And that suits you?"

"That suits me just fine."

"Here ya go, Mr. Adams." Billy set their plates down in front of them. "Fresh beers?"

"Yeah, Billy, thanks," Clint said.

The young waiter left. McBeth cut into his steak, stuck a huge chunk into his mouth. He chewed, regarding Clint across the table.

"What is it?" Clint asked.

"Adams . . ." McBeth paused. "Clint Adams. Why do I know that name?"

"Give it some thought."

They tucked into their steaks, and halfway through the meal McBeth sat back and said, "Saints preserve us."

"You got it?"

"Even as far away as Ireland we've heard of the Gunsmith," McBeth said. "I thought that draw of yours was fast. Fastest I've ever seen."

"Lots of fast-draw artists in Ireland?" Clint asked.

McBeth laughed.

"No," he said, "not a lot."

"So wait until you see some others here," Clint said, "before you rush to judgment."

# FIVE

After the meal, both men pushed their plates away and sat back. When the waiter appeared, Clint asked McBeth, "Coffee?"

"Is it good?"

"Passable."

McBeth looked at the waiter.

"Black."

"Same as Mr. Adams," Billy said. "Comin' up."

"Well, I described Jamie to you," McBeth said. "Do you think you've seen him?"

"Can't say," Clint answered. "Big and ugly matches too many men I know. How do you expect to find him?"

"I'll find him," McBeth said. "It's what I do. I hunt men."

"Like a bounty hunter?"

"I told you," McBeth said, "I am a lawman."

"Not here, you're not," Clint said.

"That's true enough," McBeth said, "but I don't intend to take any money when I find Jamie Dolan."

"What do you intend to take?" Clint asked.

"His life."

* * *

After coffee they went out to the front desk and Clint got McBeth a room. The desk clerk—a young man named Ben who looked just like Billy, the waiter, because they were brothers—knew that Clint was friends with the owner, Lucky Hansen. So when Clint told him to give McBeth a room, he did it.

"Stow your bag in your room," Clint said, "and we can go and get you a gun."

"Why you doin' this for me, Clint?" McBeth asked.

"You're a visiting lawman from another country," Clint said. "I'm just trying to show you some hospitality."

Clint remained in the lobby while McBeth went up to his room. During Clint's wait, Lucky Hansen came out of his office. Hansen, who recently turned fifty, had been a gambler all his life. Now he was trying his hand at running a hotel—not that he was giving up the gambling.

"Where you been?" he asked Clint.

"Me?" Clint asked. "Why, Lucky, I've been out making a new friend."

"Ain't you got enough friends?"

"How many is enough, Lucky?"

"Well," Lucky said, "considerin' you'd go to the wall for a friend, I'd say you got too many already. Where'd you pick this one up?"

"The docks."

"What was he doin' there?"

"Getting off a boat from Ireland."

"An Irishman?"

"That's who usually comes from Ireland."

"And what did he do to earn your friendship and help?" Lucky asked.

"He needed a friend," Clint said. "I just decided to give him the help."

Lucky shook his head.

"Always buyin' into other people's trouble, Clint," he

said. "That's gonna get you killed one of these days. I'll lay odds."

Clint laughed.

"That's not a bet I'm willing to take, Lucky," he said. "I'm going to die from a bullet before I die in bed. I resigned myself to that a long time ago."

"Me," Lucky said, "I'm gonna die at a poker table. I prefer it to either of your options."

# SIX

Jamie Dolan flipped the girl over on her back. He didn't know what excited him more, her big tits or her split lip. He finally decided it was the split lip. God had given her the tits, but he'd given her that.

He reached down with his big hands and grabbed her breasts. He pinched her nipples, hard enough to make her bite her lip, to force tears from her eyes.

His huge penis was poking her. Her eyes were afraid. She thought he was too big for her. Surely, if he tried to put it in her it would hurt and maybe even damage her.

"Please . . ." she said.

"Please what?"

"Please . . . don't . . ."

He squeezed her breasts tighter, grinning.

"I like when they beg."

He removed one hand from her breast, slid it down her body. Even though she was small—barely five feet—she had a voluptuous body. She was like a child and a woman at the same time.

He slid his finger into her, wiggled it around. She became wet in spite of herself.

She was barely nineteen, but he knew she was no virgin

for the simple reason that she had been sent over from the whorehouse. Unless this was her first time—but he doubted it. Sure, she felt tight, but she'd been fucked before.

Only not the way she was about to be.

He grabbed her thighs, spread them open, and drove his rigid penis into her. Her eyes widened and she screamed—not from pleasure but from pain.

Which was his pleasure . . .

Later, he flipped her over again. She was limp, but it didn't matter to him. He withdrew from her, glistening with her juices. He pressed the wet tip of his penis to her ass, spread her cheeks and pushed. The spongy head spread her anus, entered, and then was followed by the hard shaft.

"Oh, God . . ." she moaned, because she was too weak to scream anymore.

He lifted her up onto her hands and knees, grabbed her hips, and began to fuck her brutally.

"There ya go," he said, with glee. "Come on, lass. Love it!"

She moaned again . . .

Dolan stood at the window of his room, looked down at the Barbary Coast. As soon as he'd gotten off the ship that had brought him here, he recognized the coast as his kind of place. Behind him the girl lay curled up on the bed, crying softly.

"Finish yer cryin', gal, then get dressed, and get out."

"I-I can't walk."

He laughed.

"I figured I fucked you stupid," he said, "but now you can't walk either?"

"N-no."

He turned to look at her. There was some blood on the sheet. Perhaps she had been a virgin, after all. Or maybe he'd just torn her up inside. He thought about killing her, but that would have started him off on the wrong foot in this new country.

"I'll go and get somebody to help you," he said. Then he laughed and added, "Wait here."

He got dressed and left the room.

In the lobby the desk clerk shuddered when he saw Jamie Dolan coming down the stairs. The man frightened him to death.

"You!" Dolan said.

"Y-yes."

"Send for someone from the whorehouse," he said. "The poor bitch can't walk." He laughed and cupped his crotch. "Ya ever fuck a gal so she can't walk, lad?"

"N-no sir."

"I didn't think so."

The clerk was about thirty, but looked younger. He also—as far as Dolan was concerned—was so slight he looked more like a girl than a man.

"I need somebody to get that gal outta my room . . . quick."

"Yes, sir."

Dolan pointed a thick finger at the clerk.

"Don't make me wait too long, boy."

"No, s-sir."

"I'm goin' back up," Dolan said. "If somebody ain't here in ten minutes ta get her, I'll toss her out the window. And then I'll come back for you. Understand?"

"I-I understand."

Dolan grinned.

"There's a good lad," he said, and then went back up the steps.

# SEVEN

"It feels odd," McBeth said.

He was talking about the Western rig sitting around his waist.

"Wear it a little lower," Clint said.

"Like this?"

"You'll be able to get it out more quickly," Clint said.

McBeth touched the Peacemaker in his holster and said, "I can see that."

"And you can stop wearing the empty rig around your shoulders."

"Yes. That would be good."

"It's getting late," Clint said. "You probably want to get some rest."

"Yes," McBeth said, "I've been on the move for a very long time."

"Tomorrow you can get some new clothes," Clint said.

"I won't need to take up any more of your time for that," McBeth said. "You must have . . . a life?"

"Well, yes, actually, I do," Clint said. "I was planning on leaving tomorrow, since the person I was supposed to meet has apparently changed his mind."

"Then you should go," McBeth said. "I'll start my huntin' tomorrow."

"Well," Clint said, "if your hunting leads you out West, we may meet again."

"And if it leads me out East?"

"Much less likely," Clint said.

"Well, then," James McBeth said, "I hope it'll lead me out West."

Jamie Dolan slammed the door to his room. The two men who had come from the whorehouse to retrieve the girl had barely gotten through the doorway in time.

He turned, looked at the bedsheet with some of the girl's blood on it. That didn't bother him. Back in Ireland he had bathed in the blood of his victims. It wouldn't bother him to sleep in it. In point of fact, he enjoyed the smell. It was sweet to him—especially the scent of a young girl's blood.

Dolan was naked. He hadn't bothered to cover himself when the men from the whorehouse arrived. Hell, they worked in a cathouse. They'd seen naked men before.

Of course, probably not like him. He looked in the mirror at himself. His chest was covered with a mat of black hair. He looked down. His penis jutted from a mass of black hair, and hair covered his legs as well. A woman had once—affectionately—called him a bear. That was before he'd fucked her and killed her.

He turned and went to the bed, lay down on his back. His penis stood straight up. Maybe he should have sent for another woman. But no, he needed to get some sleep because tomorrow he'd start his journey. The Barbary Coast had been nice, but he knew James McBeth would be on his trail, and he wasn't quite ready to face him. Not yet. There was still a lot to be done.

He reached down, stroked his thickening manhood. He didn't have time to send for a woman, so he'd have to take care of the thing himself. That was okay. He wouldn't have to get rid of the woman after.

He took care of his need, then rolled over. He hoped he'd fall asleep before the damn thing started demanding attention again.

He really had no control over it.

No control, at all.

Clint looked out the window of his own room, thinking about what Lucky Hansen had said to him about getting involved in other people's troubles.

When he saw what was happening on the dock—four against one—there was no way he could have just sat by and watched. So he dealt himself in. Then, when he found out that McBeth was a lawman—the man had shown him credentials over their meal, even though they meant nothing in this country—he felt the need to get the man properly outfitted to deal with America, and to get him a room so he could get some rest.

So that was it. He was all done. Heading out tomorrow, back to Texas. McBeth seemed to be very confident in his abilities as a manhunter. And he was old enough and experienced enough to know his own abilities. There was no need to try to help the man any further, especially since he didn't seem to want it.

Clint didn't know for sure, but he thought there was more behind McBeth's hunt than a lawman's desire to do his job. But McBeth had not confided anything to him, and why should he? They'd only known each other for one day.

So tomorrow he'd saddle Eclipse, and he and his Darley Arabian would get on with their lives.

# EIGHT

LABYRINTH, TEXAS, 3 MONTHS LATER . . .

Clint Adams sat at a back table in Rick's Place, enjoying a quiet beer. It was early afternoon and, other than him, there was only the bartender and another man standing at the bar. Rick Hartman himself—Clint's friend and the owner of the saloon and gambling hall—was nowhere to be seen. Clint knew that Rick was seeing a new woman he had hired, so it was very likely the two were still in bed in the saloon owner's room upstairs. He was tempted to go up and bang on the door, but decided to just sit and quietly enjoy his beer instead.

The man at the bar was talking loudly with the bartender, who looked bored.

"So this fella who talks funny says he's lookin' for this other fella with a funny name . . ."

"So one guy talks funny, and the other one's got a funny name?" the bartender asked.

"That's what I said," the patron said. "Ain't ya listenin', Paul?"

Clint didn't know Paul. The bartender had been hired by Hartman while Clint was out of town.

"I'm listenin', I'm listenin', Andy," Paul said. He looked over at Clint, saw him watching, and shrugged.

"So this guy, he talks real funny—"

"How funny?"

"Ya know, like he was . . ."

"What? A Chinaman?"

"Naw, not a Chinaman," the other man said. "He said stuff like *boyo*, and *ye* instead of *you*. What's that? Like . . . a . . . whatayacallit . . ."

"An Irishman?" Clint asked

Both the man and the bartender turned and looked at Clint.

"Yeah, that was it," the man said. "An Irishman."

Clint got up and carried his beer to the bar.

"And was he looking for another Irishman?"

"Well . . . yeah, he was," the man said. "Said he was trackin' him, but I didn't see this Irish guy as much of a tracker."

"And where was this?" Clint asked.

"Over around Kerrville," the man said.

Kerrville was not far from Austin, north of Labyrinth.

"What's your name?"

"Me? I'm Andy Martin."

"Andy, when was this?" Clint asked. "That you saw this man there?"

"A few days ago," the man answered. "I only noticed him because of that funny accent."

"That's all?"

"Well," the man said, "he was also always playing with his gunbelt. Ya know, always kinda hitchin' it up, like it didn't fit?"

"I see," Clint said. "And he said he was hunting someone?"

"He was askin' around town about him," the man said, "so yeah, he was huntin'. Musta been some kinda bounty hunter, though, 'cause I didn't see no badge."

Clint nodded, told Paul to give him another beer and one for the stranger.

"Hey, thanks, mister," the other man said.

"Don't mention it."

Clint turned to carry the new beer back to his table. While he'd been talking, Rick Hartman had arrived and seated himself at Clint's table.

"Didn't see you," Clint said when he reached the table. "Want a beer?"

"No," Hartman said, "Paul will bring me some coffee. Have a seat and tell me about this fella with the funny accent, and why you're so curious."

Clint sat.

"How much did you hear?"

"Enough to know that you're gonna go off traipsin' after somebody else's business again."

"Remember when I was in San Francisco about three months ago?"

"Oh," Hartman said, "that fella. The one just off the boat?"

"Sounds like him."

"So he made it as far as Texas, huh?"

"I guess so," Clint said. "He's still hunting his man."

"If it's the same man," Hartman said. "Maybe he's just huntin' for a livin'."

"It was my impression that as soon as he caught his man he'd head back to Ireland," Clint said, "so my guess is it's the same man he's after."

"That makes him one stubborn lawman," Hartman said, "tracking a man for three months."

"Yeah," Clint said, "he struck me as the stubborn type."

"So what are you gonna do?" Hartman asked. "Take a ride up to Kerrville?"

"Why not?" Clint said. "I'm getting antsy anyway."

# NINE

It was two days later when Clint entered the saloon where Andy Martin said he'd heard the "funny-talkin' Irishman."

Kerrville looked to be a thriving community that was still growing. Clint liked Labyrinth because it had found its comfortable size and was satisfied with it. Of course, the day somebody came to town with some money and imagination, that would probably change. That's when he'd find a new place to hang his hat when he wasn't in the saddle.

It wouldn't be Kerrville, though. This town was still growing, and growth brought growing pains.

He entered the saloon and walked to the bar. At this time of day the bar was half full.

"Help ya?" the bartender asked.

"Beer," Clint said, "and some information."

"Beer I got," the barkeep said. "Don't know about information."

He went and got the beer, came back, and set the frothy mug down in front of Clint.

"What kind of information?"

"You had a fellow in here . . . oh, maybe five days, a week ago."

"Lots of fellas in and out of here in that time," the man

said. "What makes you think I'd remember one in particular."

"This one spoke with an Irish accent," Clint said, "and was looking for another man who spoke with an Irish accent."

"Oh," the bartender said, "them."

"You saw both of them?"

"Not at the same time," he said. "One of 'em was in here a couple of weeks ago. Had some men with him. They was a mean bunch, is why I remember 'em. Also had a little set-to with the law here."

"About?"

"Might wanna talk to the sheriff about that," the bartender said. "Now, that second fella, he come in here alone, lookin' for the first one. Seems like they was from the same country. I tol' him what I tol' you, but I also tol' him that the other fella wasn't alone."

"And?"

The bartender shrugged. "He didn't seem to care."

"Did he talk to the sheriff here?"

The bartender shrugged.

"Who is the sheriff?"

"Fella name Barfield," the barkeep said. "Been wearin' the tin around here for about six months or so."

"Got deputies?"

"Had one," the man said. "That's probably what you should be talking to him about."

Clint drank down half the beer and said, "Thanks."

"Sure thing."

He started to leave, then turned back to the bartender, who answered his question before he could ask it.

"Go out the door, make a left, and walk three blocks," he said. "Ya can't miss it."

"Thanks again."

Clint left and headed for the sheriff's office.

* * *

Hanging outside the sheriff's office was the biggest placard Clint had ever seen bearing the name of the local sheriff. The sign hung from two chains so that it would swing in the wind. It almost looked like an advertisement for something, but it only read SHERIFF WILLIE BARFIELD.

When Clint entered he thought the man seated behind the desk looked as if he'd stepped out of a painting. His shirt was dark blue, and the neckerchief around his neck was red. He had a well-cared-for mustache that flipped up on the ends, and a healthy red to his cheeks. He stood as Clint approached, appeared to be a lanky six feet and about thirty years old.

"Can I help you, sir?" he asked.

"Yes," Clint said, "my name's Clint Adams. I'm looking for a man who was in your town about five days ago, an Irishman who was looking for another Irishman."

"Irishman," the sheriff repeated, seeming to study on it.

"Yes," Clint said. "His name was James McBeth and he may have been looking for a man named Jamie . . ." Clint tried to conjure up the last name, and then did so. ". . . Dolan."

"The Dolan Gang," Sheriff Barfield said, narrowing his eyes. His hand hovered over his holstered gun which, Clint noticed, had a pearl handle. "What's your connection with them?"

"I have no connection," Clint said. "In fact, I didn't even know there was a Dolan Gang. I'm looking for the man who is tracking Jamie Dolan. His name is McBeth."

"I don't know no McBeth, but there was another Irishman here last week lookin' for Dolan."

"What'd you tell him?"

"I tol' him what I'm tellin' you," Barfield said. "You'd better not have no connection with them boys. They shot my deputy."

So that was what the bartender meant when he said they had a "little set-to" with the law.

"I already told you my name, and that I'm not connected with any gang," Clint said. "Do you know where McBeth—the other Irishman—went when he left here?"

"No idea," the fancy-dressed Barfield said.

"Sheriff," Clint said, "it's not a good idea to have your hand hovering over your gun like that, unless you mean to use it."

"Oh, I mean to use it, all right," Barfield said, "if I have to." He stuck his jaw out. "You got somethin' else to say?"

"No," Clint said, shaking his head, "I think you and me have talked enough."

With such an attitude, if Barfield had come up against a gang, it was a wonder only his deputy got shot.

# TEN

Clint turned to leave, then froze when the lawman said, "I think you'd better hold it."

Clint turned and looked at the man. The sheriff had drawn that pearl-handled revolver and was pointing it at Clint.

"What?"

"I let that Irishman walk out of here too easy," Barfield said. "I ain't gonna make the same mistake twice."

"Believe me, Sheriff," Clint said, "you're making an even worse mistake now."

"That's what you say," Barfield replied. "Take off that gunbelt."

Clint turned to face the lawman full on.

"I don't think so."

The lawman frowned.

"Why not?"

"You've got no cause to detain me or take my gun," Clint said.

"I got all the cause I need, right here," the lawman said, tapping his badge with his left hand.

"Sheriff," Clint said, "I don't know how you got this job, but you're not going to keep it long with plays like that. In fact, you try this on the wrong guy, you won't last long, period."

"You threatenin' me?"

"You got that backward," Clint said. "You've got your gun out, which means you're threatening me."

"Look, Mr. Whatever-your-name-is—"

"You weren't listening," Clint said. "My name is Clint Adams."

He studied the lawman's face as Barfield thought . . . and then it dawned on him. Suddenly, he licked his lips and looked at his gun nervously.

"I-I didn't realize . . . I didn't hear you when you first—"

"I know you didn't," Clint said. He reached out, put his hand on the man's gun, and pushed it down so that it wasn't pointing at him anymore. "You've got to learn to listen more closely."

"Yeah, I guess."

"What happened when the Dolan Gang came to town?" Clint asked.

"They were mean," Barfield said. He sounded like a schoolboy. "Pushin' people around on the street, threatenin' men in the saloon. My deputy braced them and they shot him."

"Dead?"

"No," Sheriff Barfield said, "he's laid up. But when he gets back on his feet, he sure won't want to wear a badge again."

"Probably smart," Clint said. "Might be something for you to think about."

The man's shoulders drooped and he holstered his gun.

"I-I always wanted to be a lawman," he said, "but . . ."

"You're not cut out for the job."

"W-why do you say that?"

"Well," Clint said, "first the clothes, then the gun . . . and I'm sure there's a lot more. Think it over."

"Yeah, well . . ."

"You sure you don't know where McBeth was headed?" Clint asked.

"Who?"

Clint shook his head, patted Barfield on the shoulder, and said, "Think long and hard about changing jobs."

# ELEVEN

Clint decided to stay at a hotel for one night, see what he could find out in town. He started by putting Eclipse in a livery, then asking the liveryman about anyone with an Irish accent.

"Irish," the old man said. "I got no use for Irish. Yeah, there was one here last week."

"And you haven't seen any others?"

"No," the man said, "if there was another one, he musta put his horse someplace else."

"Did the man say where he was going, or which way he was heading, when he left?"

"He didn't talk to me," the old man said. "He just came, got his horse, and left."

"You didn't see which way he went?"

"I just went back to work, mister," the liveryman said. "I don't go and check to see which way my customers go when they leave here. Far as I'm concerned, that's their business, ain't it?"

"Yep," Clint said, "it sure is."

Clint turned to leave and the man called, "Wait a minute."

"What is it?"

The old man came closer.

"The Irishman, he had me re-shoe his horse while he was here."

"And?"

"The shoes I used were ones I had taken from another horse that died," the man said. "They were new, so when the animal . . . well, anyway, I sold them to the Irishman and reused them."

"And?" Clint said again.

The old man walked away, came back with a plain shoe.

"The ones I gave him have a small triangle—here." He showed Clint the spot, at the very bottom of the U-shape. "Anybody wanting to track this man would have no problem, I think."

If McBeth had been the one being tracked instead of the man doing the tracking himself, Clint might have thought the old liveryman had marked him deliberately.

"Why would someone make shoes that were marked like that?" he asked.

"I don't know," the man said. "It might have been the duplicate of a brand."

Clint looked down at the ground. If there were any of McBeth's tracks there, they had long since been trampled, but outside of town it would be a different story.

"Okay, Pop," Clint said. "Thanks."

"Yeah, sure."

Clint left the livery.

He found a poker game that night, played quietly, and listened to the men at the table talk to one another. Clint also eavesdropped on conversations going on around him. Nobody mentioned an Irishman.

Toward the end of the night, though, he was standing at the bar after having won fifty dollars in the small poker game when a girl standing near him mentioned an Irishman.

". . . big, and mean," she said, talking to another girl. "And he liked hurtin' me. I was sore for days."

"Excuse me," Clint said.

The girl speaking was a short blonde. When she turned, Clint saw that she was very buxom. The girl she was talking to was tall and dark-haired, with a nose that was a little too big for an otherwise lovely face.

"Want some company, honey?" the dark-haired girl asked.

"No, thanks," Clint said, "I couldn't help overhearing what your friend, here, was saying."

"I got work to do," the dark-haired girl said, and left.

"The Irishman you were talking about," Clint said to the blonde. "When was he here?"

"I don't know. A couple, maybe three weeks ago."

"Not last week?"

"No," she said, "definitely not last week." She laughed. "If it was, I'd still be sore."

"Can you tell me what he did to you?"

She looked around, almost shyly, and then said, "Well . . . not here."

"Look," he said, "it's important. Where can we talk?"

"Where are you staying?"

"At the hotel right across the street."

"A-all right," she said. "I'll come to your room when I'm finished here. It'll be later, though."

"That's okay," Clint said. "I'll be awake. What's your name?"

"Eve."

"My name's Clint," he said.

"I'll see you in a couple of hours, Clint."

"Thanks, Eve."

He left the saloon and went to his room to wait.

# TWELVE

Clint was reading when the knock came at the door to his room. As always, he answered it with his gun in his hand. When he opened it, Eve slipped in very quickly and pushed the door shut behind her.

"Worried somebody will see you?"

"We're only supposed to . . . entertain in the saloon upstairs," she said. "I just don't want to get in trouble."

"I don't want to get you in trouble, Eve," he said, putting the gun in the holster on the bedpost. "I'll pay you for your time, if that makes a difference."

"Well . . . you just wanna talk, right?"

"That's right."

She shrugged, and her big breasts jiggled. She was still wearing her work clothes, a low-cut red gown.

"It wouldn't be right for me to take money just for talkin'," she said.

"I don't have a problem paying," he said, "you shouldn't have a problem taking it."

"Are you . . . on the run?" she asked. "Is that why you answer the door with your gun?"

"No," he said, "I'm not on the run, I just have to be careful. But the big Irishman you were talking about, he was on the run, right?"

"He didn't say so," she said, "but I heard him talkin' to some of his men, and that's the impression I got."

"And you didn't talk to an Irishman last week?"

"I didn't say that," she said. "I said he wasn't the one who hurt me. He wasn't even with me."

"But he talked to you?"

"Yeah," she said, "he talked to everybody."

"Okay," he said, "let's talk about the first Irishman first . . . the big one."


The Dolan Gang consisted of Jamie Dolan, Ed Grey, Billy Ludlow, and a Mexican named Santee. They were camped for the night somewhere near El Paso, with intentions of crossing into Mexico the next day.

Santee was a cold-blooded killer who liked to use a knife. He was the first one Dolan hooked up with when he left San Francisco. He was also the cook.

"Chow's on," Santee called.

The other three came over, picked up plates and held them out. They also filled their tin coffee cups. Then they went and sat down with their food. Santee, as always, served himself last, then went and sat by Jamie Dolan.

"Good chow, like always, Santee," Dolan said.

"Bacon an' beans," Santee said. "Nobody can ruin bacon and beans."

"When are ya goin' to make some potatoes, though?" Dolan asked.

"You Irish an' your potatoes."

"Yeah, you Mexicans and your—what are they called? *Frijoles?*"

"Yes, *frijoles*."

"Why don't you make us some *frijoles* some time?" Dolan asked.

"I would make some tortillas," Santee said, "but those two will not appreciate them."

"Yeah, I know," Dolan said. "All they know is bacon and beans. Well, when we get to Mexico they're going ta have to eat Mexican food, aren't they?"

"*Sí*," Santee said, "they are."

"Well then, better get 'em used to it," Dolan said. "To-morrow make us some Mexican food."

"We will need supplies."

"We'll stop and get them, boyo."

"What about your . . . countryman?" Santee asked. "He is still on our trail, no?"

"He is still on our trail, yes," Dolan said. "How do they say it in this country? There is *no quit* in James McBeth."

"That is not the kind of man you want hunting you down, *senor*."

"Well, my friend," Dolan said, slapping the Mexican on the back, "I don't think we want any man hunting us, but such is the nature of our business."

Santee turned and looked over his shoulder at Grey and Ludlow.

"How long will we keep them with us?"

"Not long," Dolan said. "We'll find better."

Dolan and Santee had met in a bar fight in a Nevada town, and during that short fight they'd saved each other's lives and formed a bond—and, at the same time, the Dolan Gang. They'd been hitting banks and stagecoaches ever since, usually with two other men, but they still hadn't found two men they'd keep with them steady.

"We'll get rid of them in Mexico somewhere," Dolan said. "Maybe you have some *compadres* who might ride with us?"

"I might, *senor*," Santee said, "I might. More coffee?"

"Hell, yeah," Dolan said. "Drinkin' your coffee is better than bein' with a two-dollar whore."

* * *

Also camped for the night, several days behind the Dolan Gang, was James McBeth.

During the three months he'd been in the United States McBeth had become more comfortable with his American clothes, saddle, and gun—although he could never get the holster to sit comfortably on his hips.

There were two things that were plentiful in the United States that he had not availed himself of: whiskey and whores. He felt that either would dull his senses and he knew he needed to be sharp to find Jamie Dolan and then kill him. Especially now that Dolan had aligned himself with others and rechristened himself as the leader of the Dolan Gang.

If Dolan now thought of himself as Jesse James or Billy the Kid, McBeth was bound and determined to see that he suffered the same fate.

# THIRTEEN

"I'm not sure what his name was," Eve said, sitting on the bed. "All I know is he was . . . huge." Her eyes widened. "I mean, he was a big man, and all, but—down there, he was . . . huge."

"Did it hurt?"

"Well, it was . . . I wasn't sure how it would feel. I've never been with a man that . . . big."

"Okay," Clint said, "I get it, he was big."

"But he was mean," she said, shuddering. "He likes to hurt people."

"And he hurt you."

"He hurt my . . . my breasts," she said. "He squeezed them, he pinched them, left marks behind, you know? And I was sore for a week. He also split my lip when he slapped me, made my head ring . . ."

"Couldn't you call for help?" Clint asked. "Doesn't the saloon supply that kind of help?"

"I thought he would kill me if I screamed," she said. "And I know he woulda killed the bouncers. They never would've been able to handle him."

"Let me get this straight," he said, sitting next to her.

"You took a beating so that your bouncers wouldn't get killed?"

She smiled wanly.

"You make me sound so noble," she said. She sighed and leaned her head against his shoulder. He turned his head and found himself looking down her impressive cleavage. He could feel the heat rising from her, and his body responded.

"I was just afraid," she said. "I'm used to men treating me without love, like a piece of meat, rutting and rolling off."

He put his arm around her and she snuggled closer.

"So while he was hurting you was he saying anything?" Clint asked.

"He was telling me how much he liked it," she said. "He'd flip me over on my stomach, then on my back again. He'd growl like an animal. And he was hairy like an animal. A-at one point I really thought he was going to kill me, and he looked . . . happy about it."

She shuddered and he pulled her close to him. She had perfumed her cleavage and the pleasant scent wafted up at him.

They sat that way for a while and then she sighed and tilted her head up to look at him. She had a small, full-lipped mouth and when he leaned down to kiss her, her tongue blossomed into his mouth.

"You deserve to be treated with kindness," he told her. "And love."

"I'm a whore," she said. "I'll settle for kindness."

"You shouldn't have to settle for anything."

He pulled her up so she was in his lap, straddling him, and kissed her soundly. She put her arms around his neck and pressed herself to him tightly. They kissed that way for a while and then she pulled her head back and looked at him.

"There's no charge for this, you know."

"Hush," he said.

He unzipped her dress in the back and pulled it down to her waist. Her breasts spilled out. He took them in his hands, lifted them to his mouth, and nuzzled her already distended pink nipples. She took some pins out of her hair and shook it free so it fell down past her shoulders.

"What a beautiful creature you are," he said into her cleavage. "And so sweet."

"Oh, my God," she said, "I believe you're the only man who could ever make me come with words!"

"Well," he said, laughing, "let's see if we can't use a little more than that."

# FOURTEEN

Eve held the back of Clint's head while he worked over her breasts with his mouth, tongue, and teeth. She wiggled her butt, enjoying how hard his cock felt in his pants.

"Oooh, God," she said, "I want to get that thing out of your pants."

She stood up, pulled her dress down, and stepped out of it. When she was naked—the hair between her legs plentiful and even blonder than the hair on her head—she undid his belt and unbuttoned his trousers. He lifted his hips so she could slide his pants off and toss them away. Since he'd been reading on the bed, he'd already removed his boots.

When his penis came into view—rigid, red, ready, willing, and able—she said, "Oh, my God."

"Maybe not as big as the Irishman's," he said.

"Oh, his was so ugly," she said, "all veiny and . . . crooked. Yours is . . . it's . . . beautiful."

She took it in her right hand, slid her hand up and down.

"It's so smooth," she said, getting down on her knees between his legs. She rubbed his column of flesh against her cheeks, then licked until it was good and wet. That done, she opened wide and took him in her mouth. Clint caught his breath and let it out slowly as she started to suck him noisily.

He watched as her head bobbed up and down. She sucked with her mouth, stroked with her hand, and before long he had to pull her off him or it would have all been over much too soon.

He put her on her back on the bed—mindful to do it gently—then lowered himself between her legs to go at her avidly with his mouth. When she was gasping and heaving about on the bed, he slid up onto her and into her and began to ride her. She dug her nails into his ass and tried to pull him into her more tightly.

"I know what I said before," she said into his ear, "but I'm not gonna break, Clint. I promise. Come on . . . harder!"

From that point on he stopped treating her like some sort of porcelain doll that might shatter and by the end they were both whooping and hollering and having a good time. . . .

Clint and Eve lay there together, catching their breath, her hand on his thigh.

"Oh, my," she said. "I never thought I'd come across a real man. Not in this town."

"Glad to oblige," he told her.

"You know," she said, "when I came up here I didn't expect this."

"Neither did I."

She propped herself up on an elbow. He stared at her big breasts.

"Did I tell you anything helpful?"

"Did you talk to the Irishman who was here last week?" he asked.

"I did," she said. "I told him about the first Irish man— the big mean one. But I couldn't tell him anything about where he and his friends were going."

"Were they his friends," Clint asked, "or his men?"

"One—a Mexican—he acted like they were friends," she said. "They sat together, but the others sat at another table. I guess they were just working for the Irishman."

"And did anyone else talk to the nice Irishman last week?" he asked.

"Jean did."

"Jean?"

"The dark-haired girl you saw me with."

"Ah."

"He didn't go upstairs with her, though," she said. "Kind of got her mad." She giggled. "Actually, I didn't mind seein' that. She thinks she can get any man she wants."

"So he proved her wrong."

"Yes."

"But they did talk?"

"Oh, yes, for a little while," she said. "Made her madder that she actually spent time workin' on him."

"She doesn't strike me as the pleasant type."

"She's only nice until she gets what she wants," Eve said, "and then she's back to bein' a bitch."

"Well, I guess I'll have to talk to her tomorrow before I leave."

"You're leavin' town tomorrow?"

"Yes."

"That soon?"

"I'm afraid so."

"Why are you tryin' to catch up to this man?" she asked. "Is he a friend of yours?"

"Not exactly."

"Then why?"

"He's a visitor to our country," Clint said. "I'm just try-ing to keep him from getting killed."

"Well," she said, sliding her hand down over his belly,

"before you go and help him, could you show me a little more hospitality?"

He smiled as she closed her hand over him.

"It would be my pleasure, ma'am."

# FIFTEEN

The next morning Eve—with malicious delight in her eyes—volunteered to wake Jean up. Clint had to speak to her while she held her wrap closed, shading her eyes from the morning light and stifling yawns the whole time.

"No," she said, "the guy would not come upstairs with me. He only wanted to know about the other man, the big one who hurt Eve."

"And what did you know about him?"

"Nothing," she said, yawning. "Only what Eve told me. That he was mean."

"What about the other men with him?" Clint asked. "Did any of them go with you?"

"Yeah," she said, leaning on her hand, "the Mexican."

"And what did he have to say?"

"*Sí* and no, mostly," she said.

"Nothing about where'd they'd been," Clint asked, "where they were going?"

"Naw," she said, "he was too smart, that one. Wouldn't say a word except what he wanted me to do."

"Okay," Clint said. "Thanks. You can go back to bed."

Jean didn't have to be told twice. She got up and dragged her rather skinny ass back up to her room.

Eve walked Clint outside.

"If you're ever back this way," she said, "make sure you stop in."

"I will," he said. "You'd better go get some rest, too, like your friend."

"Can I tell you a secret?" she asked.

"What's that?"

"She's no friend of mine," Eve said. "I hate that bitch. It was a pleasure to drag her out of bed."

She kissed his cheek and he said good-bye and walked to the livery.

"Look," the liveryman said, pointing to the ground in one of the stalls. "I found this yesterday."

Clint looked and saw a track in the dirt—a track with a triangle on the shoe.

"I just found one," the man said, "but that's what it looks like."

"Okay," Clint said, "now I know."

"You ain't gonna find any in town."

"That's okay," Clint said, mounting Eclipse. "I should be able to find something outside of town."

"Chow!" Santee called.

Once breakfast and coffee were done, Ed Grey and Billy Ludlow went off by themselves, leaving Dolan and Santee by the fire.

"Why do we not just lie in wait for him?" Santee asked.

"For McBeth? Naw." Dolan shook his head.

"Why not?"

"I don't want to make it easy on the lad. If he wants me, he's going to have to work for it."

"So we allow him to follow us into Mexico?"

"Yes."

"This man, he is very determined."

"He is, indeed."

"Is there a reason for that?" Santee asked.

"Yes," Dolan said.

He said no more.

McBeth made himself some coffee and had a breakfast of beef jerky. He wasn't keeping a cold camp exactly. It was just easier for him.

Afterward he kicked the fire to death and saddled his horse. The animal was a steeldust he had picked up after his last horse died. This was the fifth animal he had been through since getting off the boat in San Francisco. He generally rode them into the ground.

He hitched up his uncomfortable holster, mounted the horse, and headed south.

As soon as he cleared town, Clint started checking the ground for tracks. There was a trail in and out of town, but it was well-traveled and any tracks that might have been left there five days ago were gone.

But a gang trying to avoid being seen would not follow a well-traveled trail, so he left the trail and started studying the ground. It took a couple of hours but he finally found a track with a triangle on it. Then he found another. Then he found enough to give him a direction.

South.

"Damn it!"

The direction he had come from.

# SIXTEEN

Clint Adams stopped in El Paso, got a hotel room, and, over a supper of tortillas, enchiladas, and refried beans, tried to decide if he wanted to pursue the two Irishmen into Mexico. He didn't know if he wanted to take part in their little dance quite that badly. Still, McBeth was one man trailing four. The odds were stacked against him coming out of this alive.

While he was eating, a man with a badge walked in, looked around, spotted him, and came walking over. He stopped in front of Clint's table, his thumbs hooked into his gunbelt.

Last time he'd been in El Paso was before Dallas Stoudenmire had been killed. Since then, quite a few lawmen had been killed in El Paso, including some who were killed by other lawmen.

"Clint Adams?" the man asked.

"Yes?"

"I'm Deputy Marshal Ben Weaver, part of the El Paso Police Department."

"Part of it?" Clint asked. "How big is the police department?"

"Six deputies in addition to Marshal Turner."

"Isn't that a little extreme for a place the size of El Paso?"

"Not the way things have been going lately," the man said. "Mind if I sit?"

"I don't mind at all. Tequila?"

"I'll have some coffee," the deputy said.

"That's what I'm having."

Clint waved the waitress over, got another pot of coffee and another cup.

"What can I do for you, Deputy?" Clint asked.

The man sipped his coffee before answering. He looked to be about thirty-five, medium height with a well-kept mustache. He wore his holster way too high, which made Clint wonder if he knew what to do with his gun. His shirt was spotless, and his badge shiny.

"You can tell me what brings you to El Paso."

"Just passing through."

"On your way to where?"

"El Paso del Norte." Which was across the border in Mexico.

"You wouldn't be on the trail of somebody in particular, would you?"

"Like who?"

"The Dolan Gang?"

"Why would you ask that?" Clint said. "And how did you know I was here anyway?"

"You were recognized when you arrived, and I was told you were eating here."

"And what makes you think I'm after the Dolan Gang?" Clint asked.

"They rode through here about ten days ago," the deputy said. "Shot the place up, killed two of our deputies."

"So you're two deputies short right now?"

"No, we replaced them."

"And did you go after them?"

"We did, but they crossed into Mexico."

"I still don't understand why you think I'm after them."

"Why else would you be here?"

"Like I said, Deputy Weaver, I'm passing through."

"What about the other Irishman?"

"Which one?"

"His name is McBeth. He was here about four days ago, looking for the Dolan Gang."

"And what did you do to him?"

"Well, at first we arrested him."

"Why?"

"With that accent—same as Dolan's—we thought he was part of the gang."

"And he was able to convince you otherwise?"

"After a while he convinced the marshal he was after Dolan, and not part of his gang."

"And where did he go?"

"Into Mexico, after the gang."

"Alone?"

"Yes," the deputy said. "He said he preferred to work alone."

"But none of you offered to go with him anyway, did you?"

"We don't have jurisdiction across the border," Weaver said. "Maybe in del Norte he got someone to go with him."

"And do they have a police department of six deputies and one marshal over there, too?"

"No," Weaver said, "as far as I know they've got *El Jefe*, and that's it."

Clint had the feeling he was going to like *El Jefe* better than Deputy Ben Weaver.

# SEVENTEEN

After he finished eating, Deputy Marshal Weaver escorted Clint to the police department, where Marshal Sam Turner was waiting for him.

Turner was a big man—wide shoulders, big belly, mid-fifties—who stood and shook hands with Clint when Weaver brought him in.

"I know you, don't I?" Clint asked.

"You have a good memory," the man said. "Fifteen years ago, when I was with the Texas Rangers."

"That's right," Clint said. "That little scuffle in Matagorda."

"Little scuffle, he calls it," Turner said. "We killed ten desperadoes and arrested twice that many."

"That was a lot of years ago."

"And a lot of pounds," Turner said. "Have a seat. That's all, Ben."

"Yes, sir," Weaver said, and withdrew.

The brick police department building was impressive. There were two levels, the office downstairs and the cell block upstairs.

"Looks like you're doing okay for yourself," Clint said.

"After Stoudenmire's reign of terror, they decided they wanted a police department."

Clint didn't comment on Dallas Stoudenmire's "reign of terror." He'd been fairly friendly with the man.

"Still don't understand what I'm doing here, Sam," Clint said.

"Well, Deputy Weaver might have got a little overzealous, Clint, but it's still a coincidence you showin' up here on the heels of McBeth, who's trailin' the Dolan Gang."

"Far as I know McBeth is after Dolan, has been since they both were in Ireland."

"Then you do know him?"

"Met him when he got off the boat three months ago in San Francisco," Clint said, "but I haven't seen the man since."

"So you ain't runnin' with him?"

"Not with him . . . what? Four days ahead of me?"

"So this is a coincidence?"

"Pure and simple."

"What's in Mexico for you then?"

"Spicy food, spicier women."

Turner sat back in his chair, which protested beneath his bulk.

"So you're leavin' El Paso tomorrow?"

"Goin' right across the bridge to El Paso del Norte," Clint replied.

"And then?"

"On deeper into Mexico."

"It ain't exactly safe, ya know?"

"I'll look out for myself, Sam."

Turner regarded him quizzically for a few more moments, then stood up and said, "Well, it was good to see you again after so long."

Clint shook hands with the man.

"Tell me, Sam," he said, "did you bring McBeth in here for a little talk?"

"I did."

"Did he mention me at all?"

"Not once."

"But you still felt you had to bring me in."

"I don't believe in coincidence," Turner said. "Fact is, I sorta remember the same thing about you."

"As you get older," Clint lied, "you learn to tolerate them a little more."

"Maybe," Turner said. "Stop in again on your way back, Clint. We'll catch up over a cold *cerveza*."

"You got a deal, Sam."

Outside the building Clint found Deputy Weaver waiting for him.

"Mind if I talk to you, Mr. Adams?" the deputy asked.

"Thought you did that."

"Naw, this ain't official."

"Okay," Clint said. "I'm walking back to my hotel."

"I'll walk with ya."

Clint shrugged and they started walking.

"What's on your mind?"

"I wanna go with you."

"Where?"

"Into ol' Mexico."

"Why?"

"That lawman from Ireland? McBeth? He's gonna need help. You're gonna help 'im, right?"

"What makes you say that?"

"What the marshal said about coincidence."

"You always eavesdrop on your boss?"

"Every time," Weaver said. "Only way for me to learn somethin'."

"Then you heard me tell him I was just passin' through."

"I heard it."

"You don't believe it?"

"No, sir."

"Why not?"

"I know a lot about you, sir," Weaver said.

"What do you think you know about me?"

Weaver ticked points off his fingers.

"You don't like whiskey, only beer. You don't pay for whores. You try not to draw your gun unless you're gonna use it. And you don't believe in coincidence."

Clint stopped walking and looked at the deputy.

"Is this all written down somewhere?"

"Yes, sir," Weaver said. "Books, newspapers, magazines. I got a lotta stuff that's been written about you."

"And how much of it do you believe?"

"'Bout half."

Clint started walking again.

"Well, believe about half of that."

"The one about coincidence, though," Weaver said. "That one I believe. You don't do nothin' by coincidence. Ain't that true?"

"What about your job here?"

"It'll be here when I get back."

"Not if you wear that badge across the border."

"I'll leave the badge behind," Weaver said. "Take some time off."

"You'd still be a lawman."

"I'll quit," he said. "I can join again when I get back."

"What makes you think you'll come back if we go after the Dolan Gang?"

"Hell," Weaver said, "it ain't like they's the James or Younger boys. There's only been a Dolan Gang for a coupla months."

They reached the small hotel where Clint had taken a room.

"Whataya say, Mr. Adams?"

"Let me sleep on your request, Deputy."

"Then you are goin' after them?"

"I didn't say that, did I?"

"No, sir."

"We'll talk in the morning."

"Yes, sir."

Clint waited for the deputy to turn and walk away. When he didn't, Clint just turned himself and went into his hotel.

# EIGHTEEN

"So now we're in your country," Jamie Dolan said.

Santee nodded.

"We have been in my country for days."

Dolan had a plate of bacon and beans in his hands, a cup of coffee on the ground between his feet.

"It doesn't feel any different to me," Dolan said.

"If we were sitting out in the open in your country," Santee asked, "would it feel different?"

"Oh, yes it would," Dolan said. "If we were on Irish soil, I would know it."

"Dirt is dirt," Santee said, "and sky is sky."

"You're wrong," Dolan said. "Maybe some day I will take you to Ireland, and you'll see that you're wrong."

"We are a long way from your country, *amigo*," Santee said.

"I know it, Santee," Dolan said, "but that will not always be the case."

"Perhaps not," Santee said. "Later today we will be in Los Ninos, and you will see. Mexico is different."

Dolan grinned and said, "I look forward to it."

\* \* \*

James McBeth wished he knew the area well enough to
travel at night. That was probably the only way he'd make
up ground on Dolan and his gang. Perhaps what he should
have done was enlisted the aid of a local to show him the
way.

Maybe that was what he should do at the next town.

When Clint came out of the hotel the next day, he expected
to find the deputy waiting for him. Thankfully, he was not.

He found a small cantina for breakfast and was hoping
to saddle up and ride out of town without running into Deputy Marshal Ben Weaver.

It was not to be.

When he came out of the cantina, the deputy was walking across the street toward him, looking very intense.

"I missed you at the hotel," Weaver said.

"I know."

"So when do we leave?"

"*We're* not leaving, Deputy," Clint said. "*I* am."

"Why?" Weaver demanded. "Why won't you take me
with you?"

"Because I don't know you, Deputy," Clint said. "I can't
ride with a man, trust him to watch my back, if I don't
know him. It's as simple as that."

"The marshal can vouch for me."

"I'd have to be able to trust his opinion," Clint said. "I
can't. I don't know him either."

"B-but I can handle myself, Mr. Adams," Weaver in-
sisted. "I can."

"I'm sorry, Deputy," Clint said. "I have to go."

Clint started past the man, who bit his lip, then yelled,
"Wait!"

Clint turned. He knew what was coming. He could see it
in the deputy's eyes.

"If I outdraw you, will you take me with you?" the man
asked.

"Ben, I don't draw my gun unless I'm going to use it," Clint said. "This isn't a game."

"I gotta get out of this town, Mr. Adams," Weaver said.

"Ben," Clint said, using his name again, "you're not a kid. You want to leave El Paso . . . leave."

Weaver licked his lips.

"I-I can't." He looked ashamed. "I-I ain't never been anywhere else."

"I can't babysit you, Deputy," Clint said. "I won't get myself killed because you need help leaving town."

Clint turned and walked away. This time the deputy didn't call out to him.

# NINETEEN

In Los Ninos, Jamie Dolan had to admit that Mexico was different from the U.S. It was also very different from Ireland.

"All these dark-skinned, black-haired women," he said to Santee.

"Mexican women are the most beautiful in the world," Santee said.

"I like me some Indian women," Ed Grey said. "Nothin' like a squaw with a big butt."

Billy Ludlow said, "I like me some redheads. They got a lot of fire."

"Blondes," Dolan said, "big-titted blondes—but little ones, ya know?" He looked at Santee. "But I'm willin' to try a Mexican woman."

At that moment two young Mexican girls crossed in front of their horses, exchanged looks with the four men, then went off, giggling.

"Not those," Santee said.

"Why not?" Grey asked.

Santee looked at Grey.

"They are children."

"To you, maybe," Ludlow said. He and Grey were in

their twenties, while Dolan was a good ten years older, Santee more than that.

"You want a woman," Santee said, "not a girl. I will show you."

"This is Santee's country, boys," Dolan said. "He'll show us where to find some real Mexican women."

"Them two look fine to me," Grey said. "Come on, Billy, let's follow—"

He didn't finish his sentence. Dolan's huge right arm swept him from his horse's back. Grey fell to the ground, all the air going out of his lungs as he hit hard with his back.

"Wait for him to get his breath back," Dolan said to Ludlow, "and then meet us up the street."

"Where?" Ludlow asked.

"The cantina," Santee said.

Ludlow nodded, dismounted, and went to help Grey, who was gagging, his face turning blue as he tried to catch his breath.

"What was wrong with those two gals, Santee?" Dolan asked as they rode on.

"One of them was my daughter," Santee said.

James McBeth was a hunter, not a tracker.

He did not read sign. He put himself in place of the hunted, tried to figure out what his prey would do.

He knew Dolan would cross into Mexico from El Paso. That much made sense, otherwise why go to El Paso at all?

He searched for Dolan in El Paso del Norte for a day, and then left and headed deeper into Mexico.

Now he had two options. Keep going, or double-back along the Rio Grande and look for a place where Dolan and his men might have crossed into Mexico.

From information he had gleaned along the way, he knew that the Dolan Gang consisted of two men in their twenties and an older Mexican. It was the presence of the

Mexican that convinced McBeth that Dolan was not going to cross back into the United States—not yet.

The Mexican would take them into Mexico, show Jamie Dolan his country. McBeth knew Dolan would want to see some of Mexico before he left it.

Dolan never did anything without a reason. If he was in Mexico, he'd stay awhile.

# TWENTY

Clint went as far as El Paso del Norte, stopped there to speak to *El Jefe*, a man named Innocencio Higuera. He started by introducing himself.

"Please, *senor*, sit," Higuera said. "It is a great pleasure to meet one such as yourself. Who sent you to see me?"

Clint noticed that the sheriff's badge that the man wore was very tarnished. He didn't seem to mind, though. For one thing, he had enough shiny metal in his teeth to make up for it.

"Marshal Turner, from across the border, told me to speak with you."

"Ah, *mi amigo* Turner," Higuera said. "You know, he was once a Texas Ranger." He said this as if he was very impressed.

"I do know that," Clint said. "In fact, I knew him back then."

"Ah, then you are friends, no?"

"We are friends, no," Clint said. "We are more like acquaintances."

"I do not understand the difference, but it is of no consequence," the man said, waving away his ignorance impatiently. "Tell me, what can I do for the Gunsmith, *senor*?"

"I'm looking for a man named James McBeth," Clint said. "He is an Irishman."

"An Irishman?" Higuera frowned.

"He is from a country called Ireland."

"I know where an Irishman is from, *senor*," Higuera said with a smile. "I am simply trying to remember the name."

"He is chasing another Irishman named Jamie Dolan, if that helps."

"McBeth, Dolan," Sheriff Higuera said. "I do not know these names. James and Jamie? Those are not the same names?"

"They are not."

"It is odd, no?"

"Yes," Clint said, "it is."

"*Lo siento*," the man said. "Please, forgive me. I keep interrupting you."

"I'm just trying to find out what you know—if anything—about the two men I mentioned."

"Well, Dolan . . ." Higuera pursed his lips. "He has a gang, no?"

"Yes, he does."

"Then yes," he said, slapping the arm of his chair, "he was here, with his gang . . . oh, perhaps ten days ago."

"And the other man? McBeth."

"Searching for Dolan, yes," Higuera said, "I believe— yes, he was here perhaps four days ago."

"Did he tell you he was a lawman?"

"*Sí*, he did," Higuera said. He spread his hands in a gesture of helplessness. "Sadly, he is a lawman only in his own country. Not in yours, and not in mine. I warned him about this."

"The Dolan Gang caused some trouble in El Paso," Clint said. "Did they cause any trouble here?"

"None," Higuera said happily. "I was very pleased with their behavior, as were the people of El Paso del Norte."

"Why do you think that was?" Clint asked.

Higuera puffed out his chest and said, "I would not allow it, and I am *El Jefe* here. I believe they understood that." Higuera frowned at Clint and spoke to him as if he were speaking to a child. "You must be very firm with such people, *senor*." He even waggled an index finger at Clint. "It is all they understand."

"I suppose so," Clint said. "Well, thank you for your help."

He stood and the two men shook hands. Higuera was as tall as Clint, heavier through the chest and shoulders. His handshake was firm.

"I only hope that I have, indeed, helped you, *senor*," Higuera said. "If I have not I would be . . . desolate." He clutched his chest. Clint had still not decided if all the man's dramatic gestures were an act or not.

"You have."

"May I ask why the Gunsmith is also searching for this man Dolan?" Higerua asked. "Or is it the other man, McBeth, whom you seek?"

"I'm trying to see to it that Dolan and his gang don't kill McBeth."

"And this is your business . . . why?" Higuera asked with a shrug.

"Four-to-one odds," Clint said. "I just don't like them."

"Ah, but your friend, McBeth . . . he will like them even less, yes?"

"That is definitely a yes," Clint said.

# TWENTY-ONE

Clint finished his business in El Paso del Norte fast enough to simply mount up and continue on. He left town and continued to ride south. He'd gone only a few miles when he realized he was being followed. The terrain was rocky, sandy, not much in the way of vegetation, but there were hills and valleys. It was easy to tail someone if you rode in the valleys while your prey rode in the hills, and vice versa.

It wasn't so easy when your prey already knew you were following him and waited in one of the valleys for you.

Clint dismounted and waited. He had an idea who was tracking him, so he didn't have his gun in his hand when the rider came over the rise and started down. The rider saw Clint, reined his horse in for a moment, then continued on with a resigned slump to his shoulders.

"Did you really think you could follow me without being spotted?" Clint asked.

"I was hopin'," Ben Weaver said.

"I notice you're not wearing your badge."

"I turned it in."

"If I tell you to go back, you won't, right?" Clint asked.

"Right."

"You'll just keep following me."

"Right."

"I could kill you and leave your body here for the buzzards."

"But . . . you wouldn't do that," Weaver said a bit hopefully.

"No," Clint said. "I wouldn't."

"So . . . can I ride with you?"

Clint pointed a finger at Weaver.

"If we run into trouble, you'd better pull your weight, Weaver."

"I will."

"I'm not getting killed trying to protect you, understand?"

"I understand."

"And if you get me killed . . ."

"What?"

Clint didn't have anything to add, so he said, "I'll come back and haunt you."

"Okay."

Clint mounted up.

"Okay, come on."

They rode a few miles in silence before Weaver tired to start a conversation.

"So where are we goin'?"

Clint thought about remaining quiet, but what the hell. Talking would pass the time.

"I don't know."

"But I thought we were lookin' for—"

"We are looking for someone," Clint said, "but I don't really know where to look."

"So . . . where are we goin'?"

"Right now," Clint said, his eyes on the ground, "we're just riding, Ben. As soon as I spot something helpful, I'll let you know."

"Somethin' helpful?" Weaver asked. "Like what?"

"Have you ever tracked?"

"Well, I—"

"No, wait," Clint said, "you told me. You've never been out of El Paso."

"Well, I been on posses."

"So then you've tracked."

"Well . . ."

"Okay, you were with someone who tracked."

"Yeah."

"Well, I'm looking for a familiar sign," Clint said, "a hoofprint that I've seen before."

"How do you recognize a horse's print?"

"Usually, by the shoe," Clint said. "Something about the shoe."

"What about this one?"

"I'll show you when we find it."

"There."

It was an hour later. Clint pointed, then turned and looked up at Weaver.

"You have to dismount to see it."

Weaver dismounted, looked around nervously.

"We're not being watched, Ben," Clint said. "Nobody knows we're coming."

Weaver walked over to where Clint was crouched, looked at the track Clint was pointing at.

"There."

"What is that?"

"It's a triangle," Clint said. "See it? On the shoe."

"Who would put a triangle on a horseshoe?" Weaver asked, peering intently.

"We'll probably never know that," Clint told him, "but at least now we know we're going in the right direction."

# TWENTY-TWO

"That why you wanted to come here?" Dolan asked Santee when they were in the cantina. "To see your daughter?"

"It is one reason."

"You old bandit," the Irishman said. "I didn't think you had a heart."

"We all have hearts, *senor*," Santee said. "It is when they stop beating that we are in trouble."

"Santee, sometimes I think yer as smart as me own mother," Dolan said, laughing.

"She was a wise woman?"

"She was a dirty whore," Dolan said, "but yeah, she was a wise woman."

At that moment Ed Grey and Billy Ludlow came busting through the door. Grey's eyes were ablaze as he set them on Dolan. He came rushing across the room, but, before he could do anything stupid, Santee stood up and stopped him.

"He will kill you, Ed," Santee said. "Don't be foolish."

"I'm better with a gun than he is," Grey said.

"That is probably true," Santee said, "but Dolan is a man who kills for the pleasure of it. He would surely kill you before you could do him any harm."

"He's right, Ed," Ludlow said, coming up behind him. "Come on, let's go to the bar and get a beer."

Grey looked at Dolan, who was grinning up at him.

"Go ahead, Ed," Dolan said, "have a beer. I'm buyin'."

Grey hesitated, then allowed himself to be pulled away by Ludlow. Santee sat down.

"You plannin' on seein' the girl while we're here?" Dolan asked, as if Grey and Ludlow had never interrupted them.

"No."

"So you just wanted to lay your eyes on her?"

"*Sí.*"

"So you're not wantin' to stay here?"

"No," Santee said, "we can move on—unless you want to stay."

"Is there a bigger town up ahead?"

"*Sí*, many bigger."

"Then we'll move on," Dolan said, "but first I want to leave a message for my friend, McBeth."

"A message?"

"Yes," Dolan said, "you know a couple of good men in this town?"

"Good . . . how?"

"Oh, I don't mean religious, or anything like that," Dolan said, "I mean pretty good with a gun."

"There are a few."

"We only need two."

"You want them to kill McBeth?"

"Oh, no," Dolan said, "I am going to do that myself, for sure."

"Then what—"

"Like I said," Dolan replied, cutting him off, "I just want to leave him a little message."

Santee brought two men to the cantina to see Dolan, then joined Grey and Ludlow at the bar.

"What's goin' on?" Ludlow asked.

"I do not know," Santee said. "He wanted two men, I brought him two men."

"He gonna have them kill that lawman that's been followin' him?" Grey asked.

"He says no," Santee replied. "He says he wants to leave McBeth a message." When Santee said the name, it sounded like two names—Mack-Beth.

"He just wants to play with him a little," Ludlow said.

"If this man McBeth is the man Dolan says he is," Santee replied, "then he is sending these two *hombres* to their graves."

"These Irishmen can't handle a gun worth a damn," Ed Grey said. "They got no draw."

"It is not the man who draws his gun the fastest who lives," Santee said. "It is the man who shoots the straightest."

"Well, I do both," Grey said. "He wants that Irish lawman handled, he should leave it to me."

"Oh, he wants that one for himself."

As they watched, Dolan passed some money over to the two men Santee had brought in. They put their sombreros back on and left the cantina.

"Drink up," Santee said. "I believe we are leaving."

"Hey," Grey said, "I wanted to see about the local cathouse—"

"We ain't stayin'?" Ludlow asked.

"We are not staying," Santee said. He looked at Grey. "There will be plenty of women in the next town, Ed. Plenty of them."

# TWENTY-THREE

McBeth rode into Los Ninos and immediately felt all the eyes that were on him. It was as if the whole town had known he was coming. It was a little town, though, so maybe the danger was limited.

Sometimes McBeth wished he had some kind of badge to pin to his shirt. It would be a target to some people, but probably more of them would simply turn and walk away.

He reined in his horse in front of a cantina. From his saddle he could pretty much see every building in town. There was no sheriff's office in sight. The only building with any identifying name was the one he was in front of. Over the door was a crude sign that read CANTINA.

He dismounted, tied his horse off, and went inside.

"*Senor*," the bartender said, "welcome to Los Ninos. What will you have?"

"A beer."

The bartender filled a mug and set it in front of him.

"*Cerveza*," he said. "Anything else?"

There were several men in the cantina all watching McBeth drink his beer.

"Yes," McBeth said, "why is everyone so interested in me?"

The bartender shrugged.

"You are a stranger."

"Don't you get strangers in here?"

"*Sí, senor*, we do."

"And do they all get this much attention?"

The man shrugged.

McBeth turned and looked at the four other men in the place. They were way too interested in him. Almost as if they had been waiting for him.

It wasn't Dolan's style to set up an ambush for him. He knew when he finally caught up to the man that Dolan would face him one to one. But until then, he wouldn't put it past Dolan to test him, or play with him.

If these fellows were waiting for him, it wasn't to kill him, just maybe to slow him down.

He looked at the bartender.

"You know what is goin' on, don't you?"

"Yes, sir."

"You in on it?"

The barman licked his lips and said, "No, sir."

"All right, then," McBeth said. "You hit the floor behind the bar when everything starts."

"I got a scattergun back here," the man said. "You are welcome to it."

"That may not be a bad idea," McBeth said. "Keep it close."

"Sure thing."

McBeth turned to face the four men. . . .

One of them was named Jorge Chavez, another Eibar Rodriguez. These were the two men Dolan had hired to "slow McBeth down." Unfortunately, *slow* to these two men meant *dead*, so they got two more helpers—Lopez and Martinez—to sit with them and wait for McBeth, who Dolan had figured would arrive . . . today.

Chavez was about to signal the others to start shooting at

the Irishman's back when McBeth turned around and leaned against the bar. . . .

"You men waitin' for me?" he asked.

"Why would you ask that, *senor*?" Chavez asked.

"There's a phrase I've learned since I got off the boat," McBeth said. "*Itchy trigger finger.* You have all got it."

Chavez looked at the other men, then went for his gun. The other three followed.

McBeth turned. If the bartender had been lying to him, he would have been a dead man, but the barkeep had the shotgun ready and pressed it into McBeth's hands.

The Irishman turned and let loose with both barrels.

He didn't wait to see what the effect was. He dropped the weapon to the floor and drew his own gun. He felt something tug at his side as he fired at Rodriguez. The Mexican went back over a table, his gun flying out of his hand.

It was quiet.

The bartender stuck his head up, looked around at the four fallen men.

"*Caramba*," he said, "you got them all."

McBeth looked around. Two men who had been standing close together had been riddled by the shotgun blast. The other two men were lying on their backs.

"*Cerveza*?" the bartender asked.

"I guess I need one after that," McBeth said, turning.

But it occurred to him that two men had died from the shotgun blast, and then he had fired his pistol only once.

"*Senor!*" the bartender shouted.

Realizing he'd been a fool, McBeth heard the shot before he felt something punch him in the back. He drew his gun, turned, and fired . . .

# TWENTY-FOUR

Clint and Ben Weaver rode into Los Ninos six days later. During that time Clint found that Weaver could listen and learn if he tried. The problem was getting him to try. There were times when he'd just stare off into space, and Clint swore there was nothing going on behind his eyes.

The sooner he got rid of Weaver, the better he'd like it. He preferred the company of his horse. At least Eclipse listened all the time.

"This is nothin' but a village," Weaver said. "What are we doin' here?"

"This is where the tracks led us, remember?" Clint asked. "The tracks?"

"Oh, yeah." Weaver looked around. "But look, five buildings."

"It's a town, Ben," Clint said. "It's got a name and, look, it's got a cantina. It's a town."

As they dismounted in front of the cantina, Weaver said, "No hotel. How can anyone stay here?"

"They probably have rooms in back of the cantina," Clint said.

"We ain't stayin' here, are we?"

"I don't know, Ben," Clint said. "That all depends on what we find out inside."

"Well," Weaver said, following him in, "at least we can get a beer."

When they entered there were six other men there, and the bartender, so seven sets of eyes followed them to the bar.

*"Dos cervezas, por favor,"* Clint said.

*"Sí, senor."*

The bartender drew them each beer and set them in front of Clint and Weaver.

Clint knew before he picked it up that the beer was going to be warm. Weaver, on the other hand, didn't know until he sipped it.

"Hey," he complained, "this is warm."

"It is all we have, *senor*," the bartender said.

"Drink it, Ben," Clint said. "At least it's wet."

Clint could feel the eyes on him. Unless someone recognized him, they probably stared at all strangers who came to Los Ninos.

Still . . .

"What's the problem?" Clint asked the bartender.

*"Senor?"*

"Why is everyone staring," Clint asked, "including you?"

"Staring *senor*," the bartender said with a shrug. "I do not know—"

"Come on, bartender," Clint said. "What's going on? Or what went on?"

"Well, we did have something happen about six days ago," the bartender said, "but—"

"So now you're looking at strangers funny?" Clint asked. "All strangers?"

"Well . . . *sí, senor.*"

Clint turned and looked around. The six men looked

away—into their drinks or at the ceiling. He saw some stains on the floor that looked as if someone had done a bad job of washing them out.

Blood.

"How long ago did you say?" he asked.

"I would say six days, *senor*."

"And who was shot?"

"Five men, senor," the man said, then added, "well, uh, six."

"Six?"

"He was alone," the bartender said, "and the other men tried to kill him."

"Do you know who the five men were?"

"*Sí*," the bartender said, and reeled off the five Mexican names.

"And were they riding with an Irishman?"

"An Irishman, *senor*?"

"Never mind," Clint said. "Were they riding with a *gringo*?"

"Oh, no, *senor*, but they were paid by a *gringo*."

"And when was that *gringo* here?"

"Oh, many weeks ago.

"How many is many?"

"I would say . . . two?"

"Two weeks?"

The man nodded.

Clint asked, "That's many?"

The bartender shrugged.

"Okay, what happened to the sixth man?" Clint said.

"He killed the other five."

"And?"

"He was shot in the back."

Clint closed his eyes, then opened them and frowned.

"They shot him in the back, and then he killed them all?"

"No," the bartender said, "he shot them, but he was not

dead. When he turned around, he was shot in the back. Then he killed the last man."

"And then he died?' Weaver asked.

"Oh, no, *senor*," the bartender said. "He did not die. He has a room in the back."

# TWENTY-FIVE

When James McBeth opened his eyes, he saw Clint Adams looking down at him.

"Adams?"

"That's right."

"Wh-what the bloody hell are you doin' here?"

"Well," Clint said, "as a matter of fact, I was looking for you."

"Looks like you found me."

"Not exactly the way I expected to find you, though," Clint said.

"Not the way I expected to find myself either," McBeth said, shifting painfully. He was lying on his right side because the wound he suffered was in his back.

"Seems like you were a little careless."

Between gritted teeth McBeth said, "Guess you could say that."

"And you still are."

"What?"

"You're lying on your right side," Clint said.

"So?"

"Aren't you right-handed?"

"I am."

"You got your gun hanging on the bedpost, but can you get to it left-handed?"

"I-I'm not sure."

"You should be lying on your left side, McBeth."

"Truth be told," McBeth said, "it hurts less this way."

"It's going to hurt less when you're dead, too."

"I suppose," McBeth said. "If we're going to talk, could you sit down? It hurts to look up."

"Sure thing," Clint said. He pulled a chair over and sat down.

"Why are you lookin' for me?" the Irishman asked.

"Heard you were in Texas," Clint sad. "Thought I might be able to help."

"But we are in Mexico now."

"I sort of noticed," Clint said. "I've been following you for a while, so when I got to the border I just kept going. You're on Dolan's trail?"

"That's right," McBeth said. "Have been since San Francisco."

"So I guess he left a little surprise behind for you."

"I know Dolan," McBeth said. "Those men overstepped their bounds. At best they were only supposed to slow me down."

"Well, I guess they did that. You still got that bullet in you?"

"I'm afraid so," a woman's voice said.

Clint turned and looked at the lady who had just entered the room. She was obviously Mexican, with dark skin and wild black hair. She had a wrap-around peasant blouse and was wearing a long skirt that covered her knees.

"And how would you know?" Clint asked.

"Because I left it in there," she said, approaching the bed. "You're the doctor?"

"I am not a doctor," she said, "which is why I left the bullet in there. But I am the closest thing to a doctor this town has, which is why your friend is still alive."

She looked down at McBeth.

"How are you feeling today, Mr. McBeth?"

"All my parts are moving, Miss Hernandez."

"I told you to call me Jacinta," she said.

"Jacinta, this is Clint Adams."

"Mr. Adams," she said, looking at Clint. "Am I right that you are a friend? Or are you seeking to put another bullet into Mr. McBeth?"

"Given those two choices," Clint said, "let's say I'm his friend."

"Well, I am going to take a look at your wound, Mr. McBeth. Do you object to your friend staying?"

"Not at all."

She went around to the other side of the bed, removed the sheet from a mostly naked McBeth, and examined his wound.

"It is not infected," she said after taking off the bandage. "Let me put a clean dressing on."

"Ma'am, is he going to be all right with that bullet in there?"

"He will have to have it removed as soon as he can," she said.

"But will he be able to ride?"

"I would advise he not ride," she said, "but he has already told me he will not take my advice."

"How else will I get around?" McBeth asked. "I can't find Dolan on foot."

"And he insists he is still going to hunt for this man Dolan."

"I guess what we got here, ma'am, is a stubborn Irishman."

She finished with the dressing and stood up straight.

"He is lucky he is not a dead Irishman."

"That's not down to luck," McBeth said. "It's down to you, Jacinta."

"Do you want to try sitting up today?" she asked.

"I would love to sit up."

"Would you help me, Mr. Adams?"

"Of course."

"Let's just bring him up slowly. James, you tell me when it hurts too much."

"Don't worry," McBeth said. "You will be the first to know."

# TWENTY-SIX

Surprisingly, James McBeth felt better once he was sitting up. Well enough to eat and share a meal with Clint, who told Ben Weaver to go ahead and eat in the cantina.

They both asked McBeth's "doctor" to join them, but she said she had a baby to deliver.

"Several, in fact," she added. "I'll check in on you later. If you start to feel worse—" She stopped, then looked at Clint. "If he starts to feel bad again, help him to lie back down."

"I'll do that."

She nodded, turned to leave.

"Jacinta," Clint said.

"Yes?"

"You speak English very well."

She smiled.

"I was educated in your country," she said and left.

"She would be even more attractive," McBeth said, "if she had an Irish accent,"

"To you, maybe."

A middle-aged waitress—the owner and bartender's wife—came in with a tray of food and set it down for them. Enchiladas, beans, and rice. The smell set Clint's mouth to watering. When he tasted it, his mouth watered even more.

"This is the best meal I've had since gettin' off the boat," McBeth said.

"Might be because you're alive," Clint said, "but it *is* good."

They were both hungry so they ate in silence for a while until they were both almost done. The waitress came in and asked if they wanted more, and both said yes. They talked while they waited for her to return.

"You plan to stay on Dolan's trail?" Clint asked.

"I didn't come all this way to give up."

"The trail's liable to be cold by now."

"Well," McBeth said, "you did say you wanted to help. You could pick up the trail again."

"Maybe."

"You found me."

"I had help."

"What kind of help?"

Clint told McBeth about the triangle on the horseshoe.

"Who would put a triangle on a horseshoe?"

"The question has been asked more than once," Clint said.

"Any answer?"

"Sorry, no."

The woman returned with two more helpings.

"*Dos cervezas, por favor*," Clint said.

"*Sí, senor.*"

McBeth was staring at him.

"Beer," Clint said.

"Ah, good."

She returned with two mugs of warm beer. McBeth took a sip and made a face.

"Best we can do."

"The food makes up for it," McBeth said. "Will you stay and help me?"

"Dolan could be back in the U.S. by now," Clint pointed out.

"Then I'll follow him there," McBeth said. "Fact is, I will follow him to hell if I have to."

"Well," Clint said, "I think before I commit to anything, I'd like you to explain that."

McBeth stared at Clint for a few moments, then said, "Yeah, all right. I guess you've got it comin'."

"Is it a long story?" Clint asked.

"It's a very short story," McBeth said. "Dolan's specialty is killin' women."

"I know," Clint said, "you told me that when we first met."

"Yes, well," McBeth said, "what I didn't tell you is that he . . . he also killed my wife."

"Your wife?"

McBeth nodded.

"Yes," he said, "she was the last woman he killed in Ireland."

"I-I'm sorry," Clint said. "I didn't . . . I'm sorry, McBeth."

"Thank you."

"Has he killed any women since he's been here?"

"One or two along the way," McBeth said, "and he's hurt a few others."

"Can you prove he killed them?"

"No," McBeth said.

"So we've got nothing to turn him over to the law for when . . . if . . . we catch up to him?"

"He's got himself a few men to ride with him," McBeth said. "They're callin' themselves the Dolan Gang."

"Yeah," Clint said, "yeah, I did hear something about that."

"They robbed some stagecoaches and a bank or two," McBeth said. "So I'm sure the law will be interested in the other three."

"The other three?"

"Well," McBeth said, "I don't have any reason to kill them. I'm willin' to turn them over to the law. But Dolan . . . that's a different story."

"You intend to kill him?"

McBeth nodded.

"I intend to kill him."

"Well, if there's a bounty on him, that won't be a problem," Clint said. "But if you kill him in cold blood, somebody's going to come looking for you—somebody wearing a badge."

"That won't be a problem," McBeth said. "Dolan will face me fairly."

"You can say that, after he had you shot in the back?" Clint asked.

"That wasn't his intention," McBeth said. "The men he hired went too far. Dolan was just trying to slow me down. He knows I'm comin' for him, and he intends to face me."

"How do you know?"

"Because I know him very well," McBeth said. "I know how he thinks and I know what he'll do."

"Well," Clint said, "if that's the case, you ought to be able to predict what he'll do next."

"The problem is, he knows I know him," McBeth said. "That means whatever he does, it is guaranteed to be unpredictable."

"Then it sounds like you knowing him isn't going to be very helpful in catching up to him."

"I guess that'll be where you come in," McBeth said. "You know what I've been hearin' about ever since we last saw each other?"

"What?"

"The Gunsmith," he said. "I've been hearin' how the Gunsmith is a legend and can do anything."

"Well," Clint said, "don't believe everything you hear, McBeth."

"You know," McBeth said, "since we're going to be partners for a while, I think you should call me James. And I will call you Clint, if you don't mind."

"I don't mind," Clint said, "but—"

"You know," McBeth said, "now that I've eaten I really think I should lie back down for a while. You mind givin' me a hand, Clint?"

"No, James," Clint said, "I don't mind at all."

# TWENTY-SEVEN

As soon as McBeth's head hit the pillow, he fell asleep. Clint collected their plates and mugs and carried them out. The waitress met him halfway, said "*Gracias*," and took everything from him.

Ben Weaver was sitting at a table, finishing his own meal.

"What's going on?" he asked. "Is your friend okay?"

"He will be," Clint said. "He has a bullet in his back, down low on the left side. There's no doctor in town, so it can't be removed."

"Can he ride?"

"He shouldn't," Clint said, "but he will."

"When?"

"I don't know," Clint said. "Maybe days."

"That's crazy."

"I know," Clint said, "but he's got good cause to be crazy."

"So what do we do? Just hang around?"

"Why don't you walk around town, talk to some people," Clint suggested.

"What am I lookin' for?"

"Anyone who might have talked to Dolan or somebody

in his gang," Clint said. "There's supposed to be one Mexican in the gang. Maybe somebody in town knows who he is."

"We don't have any official standing in Mexico, Clint," Weaver said, "Why would they talk to us?"

"We don't have any official standing anywhere, Ben," Clint said. "And they'll talk to you if you make them talk to you."

"Make them . . . oh."

"Just don't kill anybody."

Clint stood up.

"Where will you be?"

"Around," Clint said. "The town's not so big that you won't be able to find me."

"What about rooms for the night?"

"I'll ask," Clint said, "but we may have to sleep in a barn or something."

"Great."

"Just go."

Weaver got up.

"I'm on my way."

Clint waited for the waitress to come to the table to clean it off.

"*Café, por favor?*" he asked.

"*Sí, senor.*"

"*Fuerte y negro,*" he told her. He'd learned years ago how to say "*strong and black.*"

"*Sí, senor.*"

When she returned with a pot of coffee, he asked, "*Habla inglés?*"

"*Sí.*"

"What's your name?"

"Angelina," she said. "Angel."

"Jacinta Hernandez, Angel," Clint said. "Where can I find her?"

"End of the street."

"End of the street?" he asked. "That's also the end of town, right?"

She smiled.

"*Sí, senor.*"

"Out the door, left or right?"

"Right."

"*Gracias.*"

"*Por nada.*"

"One more thing."

She turned and looked at him, frowning.

"*Senor?*"

"Any rooms available here?"

"*Sí, senor,*" she said. "Many empty rooms. Take your pick."

"Thank you."

Now it was her turn to ask a question.

"*Senor?*"

"Yes?"

"Perhaps you will be wanting ... some company tonight?"

She was middle-aged, but her low-cut peasant blouse and colorful skirt showed off a solid, appealing body. She also had a heavy-featured but pretty face.

"Isn't the bartender your husband?"

"*Sí, senor.*"

"I don't think so, Angel," he said. "Perhaps another time?"

"*Como quiera,*" she said. "As you wish. And your *amigo?*"

"You'll have to ask him."

She nodded, went back to the kitchen. Clint had two cups of coffee from the pot she'd brought, then stood up, walked out the door, and turned right.

# TWENTY-EIGHT

Clint was prepared to knock on Jacinta's door, but when he got there he saw there wasn't one. The building was adobe, like all the others, but from its condition he had a feeling he was looking at the oldest building in town.

He was still standing in the doorless doorway when Jacinta appeared, leading a little girl behind her.

"Mr. Adams," she said. "Is Mr. McBeth all right?"

"He's fine," Clint said. "He sat up for quite a while, then ate well. He's asleep now."

"Nina," she said to the little girl, "run along home and tell Mama you are fine."

"*Sí*, doctor."

The little girl ran past Clint and out the door.

"She calls you doctor?"

"Most of the people around here do," she said. "What can I do for you, Mr. Adams?"

"Please," he said, "start by calling me Clint."

"Very well, Clint," she said. "What can I do to help you?"

"A few weeks before McBeth got to town, four other men came to town," he said. "One of them was an Irishman, like McBeth. Another was Mexican. I suspect the other two were *gringos*."

"I remember them."

"You do?"

"In a village this small?" she said. "How could anyone not notice new arrivals."

"Did you happen to have to treat any of them for injuries?"

"No," she said. "I never met them."

"How long were they here?"

"Just overnight."

"Long enough to hire someone to shoot McBeth," Clint remarked. "Did they stay in back of the cantina?"

"They did," she said. "I'm afraid those rooms are usually empty. Those four men, then Mr. McBeth, now you and your friend, these are the most visitors we've had here in months."

"I see. So you never spoke to any of them?"

"I never had a reason to."

"Okay," Clint said. "Thanks."

He turned to leave, then stopped.

"One more questions."

"Go ahead."

"The bartender at the cantina, he also owns it?"

"Yes."

"And does he mind his wife . . . servicing the guests?"

"No," she said, "in fact, he insists on it. Why, are you interested?"

"She offered," he said, "but I turned her down. I hope I didn't hurt her feelings."

"I'm sure you didn't—but why did you turn her down? She's a beautiful woman."

"Yes, she is," he said, "but I've just never acquired the habit of paying for a woman."

"Well . . . that's admirable."

"Why do you sound surprised?"

"Well . . . for one thing . . . you're a man," she said. "And for another, it's . . . well, you're . . . you do have a . . ."

"What? Reputation?" he asked.

"Even down here in Mexico we've heard of the Gunsmith," she said.

"Perhaps," he said, "but did you ever hear that I was some kind of . . . whoremonger?"

"I didn't mean to offend—"

"No offense taken," Clint said. "Just don't believe everything you hear."

"Does that include what I hear from you?"

"Oh, no," he said. "I never lie."

"That so?" she asked. "Like I said, you are a man."

"You don't have a very good opinion of men, do you?" he asked.

"No," she said, "I don't."

Recalling that she had been educated in the United States, he asked, "Is that American men, or does that mean all men?"

She thought a moment, then said, "No, my opinion pretty much runs to all men."

"Where were you educated, Jacinta?"

"In the East."

"As what?"

"A nurse."

"Why did you decide to come here?"

"I came back here because this is where I was born. Los Ninos was always this small," she said.

"Couldn't you have made more money working in the U.S.?" he asked. "Working for a doctor?"

"A male doctor," she said. "Probably. But these people need me."

"Maybe," he said, turning to leave.

"What do you mean, maybe?" she demanded.

He looked at her over his shoulder.

"Maybe you need them to need you," he said. "Maybe this is just a place for you to hide out."

"What do you know?"

"Probably nothing," he said, on his way out the doorway. "Probably nothing at all."

# TWENTY-NINE

Clint went back to the cantina and arranged with the bartender–owner to secure two of the empty rooms for himself and Ben Weaver. Then, since he was at the bar, he ordered coffee. If he was going to drink something warm, he preferred it to warm beer.

"Would *senor* be looking for some company tonight?" the bartender asked him.

Clint looked at the man grinning at him with a couple of gold teeth glinting in his mouth. He wondered if the man had bought the gold with money he made from pimping out his own wife.

"That's all right," Clint said. "I think all I'll want to do tonight is sleep."

"It does not have to be Angel," he said. "If she is too fat or ugly for the *senor*, we can provide . . . other companionship."

"No, no," Clint said, "Angel would be fine, if I were looking for a woman, but I am not."

"A boy, perhaps?"

"I'm not looking for anyone!" Clint said forcefully. "I'm just going to sleep tonight."

"*Sí, senor*," the man said with a shrug. "As you wish."

He was finishing up his coffee when Ben Weaver walked back in.

"This *is* a small town," Clint said. "In fact, it's a village. Where have you been?"

"Doin' what you told me to do," Weaver said. "Talkin' to people."

"You want some coffee?"

Weaver made a face.

"I'd rather have warm beer." He signaled the bartender, who brought one over.

"Did you find out anything?" Clint asked.

"Well, everybody I talked to saw the Dolan Gang ride in and out, but nobody claims to have known any of 'em."

"Not even the Mexican?"

"Nope."

"They had to pass through here for a reason," Clint said. "This is an easy place to bypass."

"They were only here one day," Weaver said.

Clint eyed the bartender, who was wiping the bar with a dirty rag at the other end.

"I wonder if they stayed here," Clint said. "And I wonder if they wanted company for the night."

"This town got a cathouse?" Weaver asked. He sounded so hopeful Clint took a look at him.

"I don't know," Clint said, "but I think for a few pesos more you can get the owner's wife with your room."

"His wife?"

"The waitress."

"She's a little old, ain't she?"

"Maybe for you. Look, I've got an idea. Talk to the bartender about Dolan and his gang. See if any of them paid for some time with his wife. If they did, then we can talk to her."

"Why don't you talk to him?"

"I did," Clint said, "and I don't want to talk to him again."

"Where are you gonna be?"

"Sitting outside."

Clint pushed away from the bar.

"Hey, we got rooms?" Weaver asked.

"Yeah," Clint said, "the two at the end of the hall. I think the owner's wife is making up the beds. You could ask him that, too. Come outside after you ask him."

Clint found a rickety wooden chair and took it out with him, sat on the boardwalk in front of the cantina. The horses were still tied there. They were going to have to find a place to bed them down for the night.

He didn't want to spend any more time talking to the bartender, because every time he looked at the man's face he wanted to smash it in. He had no respect, no use, in fact, for a man who pimped out his own wife.

From his vantage point he could see practically the whole village of Los Ninos. At one end he noticed what looked like a small barn where they'd be able to rest the horses for the night. About the only building he couldn't see was the one Jacinta Rodriguez was set up in to do her doctoring—or her nursing.

Weaver came out and stood next to him.

"What?"

"He says one of the men spent the night with Angel."

"Well, guess what?" Clint said.

"What?"

He looked up at Weaver. "You're going to do the same."

# THIRTY

"You saw my husband behind the bar?" Angel asked.

"Yes," Ben Weaver said.

"He has a big belly," she said, "an ugly belly."

"Yes."

"And his *pene*," she said, stroking Weaver's penis, "it is small. He is not beautiful, smooth, and strong like you, my young *gringo*."

She sat on the bed next to him, naked. She had heavy breasts and wide hips, but her hands and mouth on his body were so knowing that he didn't care. She stroked him with one hand, fondled his testicles with the other. He was already tired out from her, but his penis became engorged at her touch, and when she leaned down and took it into her mouth again, any sign of fatigue in his body faded.

He knew that Clint wanted him to question her, but she had barely given him time to talk. When she walked into his room, it had taken her a second to get naked, and then she was on him voraciously. She undressed him, stroked his cock until it was hard, and then mounted and rode him until he exploded inside her.

Since then she had reawakened his tired body several times, and there had been no time to talk.

And this time was not going to be any different.

She got between his legs, sucking him wetly, avidly, and then she did something no other woman had ever done to Ben Weaver—no other whore anyway, since he'd been with mostly whores all his life. She took his hard cock between her pillowy breasts and rolled it there, rubbed it, kept at it until suddenly his body was jerking and spasming as he covered her breasts and chest with his sticky emission. . . .

An hour later Weaver woke to find Angel down between his legs again, sucking him awake. He wondered idly how Clint was going to react when he found out that Angel's husband didn't have to force her to have sex with other men. She was only too happy to do it.

"Okay, wait, wait, Angel," he said, pulling her off him.

"But *querido*," she said, "We are not finished . . ."

"I know we're not," he said. "Believe me, I don't want us to be finished for a while."

"Ah," she said, "you do not think Angel is too old or too fat now?"

"I never said that," he told her. "No, look, I need to ask you some questions before we, uh, get goin' again."

"Questions?"

"Yes."

She sat up. The dark brown nipples of her heavy breasts were very hard as he tore his eyes away from them to look at her face.

"A few weeks ago four men came to town," he said. "You spent the night with one of them."

"*Sí*," she said, "with Santee."

"The Mexican one?"

"*Sí*," she said. "He usually has me when he comes here."

"You mean he comes here a lot?"

"Whenever he comes to Mexico," she said.

"What is it he likes so much about this place?" Weaver asked. "Is it you?"

She ran her hand up his leg and said, "That would be very nice if it was me, but no, it is not me. It is Louisa."

"Louisa? Another woman?"

"A girl," she said, "but soon to be a woman."

"And what is it about Louisa that brings Santee back here again and again?" he asked.

Her hand reached his crotch and she took hold of him.

"She is his *hija*."

"*Hija*," he repeated. "She's his daughter?"

"*Sí*," she said, leaning down to him. She ran her tongue along the length of him, then wet the spongy head of his prick by sucking it noisily. "Is that all we have to talk about?"

"Jesus," he said, as she took him into her mouth, "there's more, but it can wait until m-morning."

# THIRTY-ONE

Clint was sitting at a table in the cantina when Weaver came stumbling out.

"Have some coffee," he said, pouring it. "You look like you need it."

Weaver sat down and said, "I can't hardly walk. That woman is . . . you can't hardly satisfy her." He sipped some coffee and shook his head. "I ain't never been with a woman like that, Clint." He leaned in. "And her husband ain't forcin' her to do nothin', believe me."

"Well, seems I misjudged one or both of them," Clint said. "What was that you said yesterday about her being kind of old?"

"That don't matter," he said. "That woman . . . she knew things."

"Experience," Clint said. "Did you happen to find out anything else while you were . . . together?"

"Oh, yeah," Weaver said, "I did. Seems the Mexican who's ridin' with Dolan is named Santee."

"What about him?"

"Apparently, they came here because Santee has a daughter living here."

"His daughter lives here?"

"That's what she said."

"And how does she know that?"

"Well, that's interesting, too," Weaver said. "See, she's the girl's mother."

"She was married to this Santee?"

"No, she's married to Carlos, the owner of this place, but years ago she got pregnant by Santee."

"Does her husband know?"

"No, he thinks the girl is his daughter."

"Her own husband doesn't know, but she told you?" Clint asked. "Why would she do that?"

Weaver shrugged.

"She likes me."

"And she doesn't like her husband?"

"Not very much."

Clint looked around to see if the husband was in earshot. At the moment he wasn't even in the room.

"So, does she know where he was going when he left here?"

"No," Weaver said. "She didn't speak to him. They never speak when he comes to town."

"What? But . . . what about the daughter?"

"He doesn't talk to her either," Weaver said. "In fact, she doesn't know anything about him."

"So, did you find out anything useful at all?" Clint asked impatiently.

"I think they're heading back to the U.S."

"Why do you say that?"

"The guy who spent the night with Angel wasn't Santee. It was another guy, but she doesn't know his name. He said they were going to look at a couple of larger towns in Mexico because the big Irish guy wanted to see them, and then go back to the U.S. That was weeks ago. They must've headed back by now."

Clint rubbed his jaw.

"I think you're right."

"So we head back to El Paso?"

"No," Clint said. "They won't go back there. I think they'll cross the border somewhere else."

"Where?"

"That's what we're going to have to figure out," Clint said.

"So when do we leave?"

"As soon as McBeth is ready to ride."

"And when do you think that'll be?"

"A lot sooner than is good for him, I'm sure."


Clint was sitting by McBeth's bed with a cup of coffee in his hand when the man woke up.

"Good morning," McBeth said, blinking rapidly.

"Thought you might need this."

"Thank you."

"Want to sit up and drink it?"

"Yes." Clint made a move to help him, but the Irishman waved him away, sat up, and accepted the coffee.

"Don't tell Jacinta, but I've been sitting up by myself for a while."

"Good for you. Want some breakfast? I think Angel is whipping up some burritos."

"In the morning?" McBeth asked, appalled.

"They've got eggs in them."

"Well," McBeth said, "on second thought, that doesn't sound too bad."

"I'll have her bring them in."

He stood up.

"Have you eaten yet?" McBeth asked.

"No, I've just had coffee."

"Join me then."

"Mind if I bring somebody else in?"

"Who?"

"The kid who's riding with me," Clint said. "Well, he's not really a kid, but he kind of is, experience-wise."

"Bring him in," McBeth said.

Clint nodded, went to get the food and Ben Weaver.

# THIRTY-TWO

Clint introduced McBeth and Weaver to each other and they had coffee and burritos for breakfast together. Clint noticed Angel making eyes at Weaver, who seemed uncomfortable with it.

"Looks like I'm missing a party," Jacinta said, walking in.

Angel sniffed loudly and left without looking at Jacinta.

"She doesn't seem to like you very much," Clint commented.

"She will like me fine next time she feels sick," Jacinta said. "And how are you feeling this morning, Mr. McBeth?"

"I am a hell of a lot better today, thanks to you, Jacinta."

She got around behind him so she could look at his wound.

"I think you are just a very fast healer, Mr. McBeth," she said. "However, you must have that bullet removed as soon as possible. There is no telling what will happen if it starts to move around in there."

"I understand."

"Will you have some coffee with us, Jacinta?" Clint asked.

"If I do," she said, "you'll have to introduce me to this handsome young man."

Both Weaver and Clint looked surprised. Clint had never thought of the young deputy as handsome.

"This is Ben Weaver," Clint said. "Ben, Jacinta Hernandez. McBeth's angel of mercy."

There was an extra cup so Weaver filled it for Jacinta and the two made eyes at each other over the rim. Angel came back in, looked at Weaver and Jacinta, and started to frown. Clint thought it would be a good idea to get Weaver out of Los Ninos as soon as possible.

"When do you think you want to ride?" Clint asked McBeth.

"I would ride tomorrow if I could," the Irishman said. "Is there any word on where Dolan might have gone?"

"We have some ideas," Clint said.

"He hasn't even walked yet," Jacinta said, "so riding is out of the question."

"Then I'll take a walk today," McBeth said. "Clint, will you help me?"

"Sure. After breakfast?"

"If you're going to take a walk," Jacinta advised, "you could use a bath, too. But don't get that wet, just yet."

"How do I take a bath without getting wet?" McBeth asked.

"Get somebody to give it to you," she said, finishing her coffee. "Maybe Mr. Adams can help you with that, too."

She gave Weaver one more look, exchanged glares with Angel, and left.

"Angel," Clint asked, "do you know someone who can give Mr. McBeth a bath?"

"My daughter," Angel said. "She can wash him down in bed with a sponge."

"That sounds good," Clint said.

"Now, wait a minute—" McBeth said.

"It's settled then," Clint said. "A walk and then a bath.

Can you please arrange that with your daughter, Angel?"

"*Sí, senor.*"

She took the empty plates and cups, gave Weaver a dirty look, and left.

"What did I do?" Weaver asked.

"She saw you and Jacinta making eyes at each other," Clint said.

"Well," Weaver said, "Jacinta was amazing. Did you get a look at her?"

"Yes," Clint said, "I did. You ready to stand up, McBeth?"

"Ready as I'll ever be."

# THIRTY-THREE

McBeth got himself dressed—was even able to pull on his boots—and then he went for a walk with Clint on one side and Weaver on the other.

"You're pretty steady," Clint said. "I think Jacinta was right. You are a quick healer. But if you're going to ride we're going to have to wrap you up tight to keep the wound from bleeding."

"You can do that," McBeth said. "I think Jacinta has done enough."

"Actually," Clint said, "if you're a quick healer she hasn't done much, has she? Couldn't remove the bullet."

"She did stitch the wound closed," he pointed out.

"Okay," Clint said, "there is that."

"Can you remove the bullet?" McBeth asked.

"I've done it once or twice," Clint admitted, "but that would hold you up for days."

"Good point."

"Might save your life, though," Weaver said.

McBeth looked at the ex-deputy, then said, "Another good point, but no. I've got to ride. If I let Dolan get too far ahead of me, he'll be bloody hard to catch."

They walked to the small barn that housed all three of

their horses. Clint checked briefly on Eclipse just for something to do, and then they started walking back.

"How you doing?" Clint asked.

"I'm actually feelin' pretty strong," McBeth said, as if he himself was surprised.

"You'd better rest the remainder of the day," Clint said.

"I want to ride out tomorrow, Clint."

"Isn't that a little soon?"

"I feel really good," McBeth said. "Let's make it tomorrow."

Weaver looked over at Clint, who shrugged.

"Why don't you and Mr. Weaver decide which way we're gonna go?" the Irishman asked. "I'll trust ye to make a good decision."

"We'll make an educated guess," Clint replied.

"I'll rest for the remainder of the afternoon, but I'll take my supper in the cantina, sitting at a table," McBeth said.

"If that's what you want," Clint said.

"That's what I want."

"Okay, then," Clint said. "We'll spend one more night here."

"Mr. Weaver," McBeth said, "the way you got them two women lookin' at you, you'd better mind how you decide how to spend the night."

"Ain't never had two women wantin' me before," Weaver said.

"I suspect Angel wants pay for another night," Clint said.

"And Jacinta?" McBeth asked.

"No telling what she wants," Clint said. "She doesn't have a very high opinion of men."

"She said I was handsome," Weaver said.

Clint looked at McBeth and said, "See what I mean?"

McBeth laughed.

McBeth rested until supper time, then came out into the cantina and joined Clint and Weaver at a table.

"First time I been in a chair since I got shot," he said.

"How's it feel?" Clint asked.

"Kind of stiff."

"Probably going to be even stiffer in the saddle," Clint observed.

"No," McBeth said, "it'll stretch out and feel better the more I ride."

"Sounds like you been shot before," Weaver said.

"Once or twice."

"I ain't never been shot."

"It isn't something to look forward to, Weaver," Clint said.

Angel came out of the kitchen with a tray.

"I took the liberty of ordering steaks," Clint said to McBeth.

"Sounds good," the Irishman said. "I think I've had enough tacos and enchiladas to last me a lifetime."

Angel laid out the plates, and three mugs of lukewarm beer to wash the food down with. She bumped Weaver's shoulder with an ample hip before heading back to the kitchen. There was a man and a woman at another table eating, and the bartender behind the bar. Other than that, nobody else was around.

"Eat up," McBeth said to Weaver. "I've got a feelin' you're gonna need your strength tonight."

Weaver picked up his knife and fork, looking uncomfortable.

# THIRTY-FOUR

In the morning Clint walked McBeth to the stable where the horses were. He saddled both McBeth's horse and Eclipse.

"Where's Weaver?" McBeth asked.

"He'll be along," Clint said.

"Which woman did he end up with?"

"I don't know," Clint said. "He said he didn't have the money to pay for Angel again."

"You think he spent the night with Jacinta?" McBeth asked.

Clint shrugged.

"If he did, I envy him," McBeth said. "That is a beautiful woman."

"She hasn't got much use for men, though."

"Still, even a woman who hates men would have one use for us . . . don't you think?"

"I don't know," Clint said. "I try not to deal with women who hate me."

"Did you decide which way we should go?" McBeth asked.

"We'll ride east, head for the river, find a likely place to cross."

"Just like that?"

"Well, they won't go back to El Paso," Clint said. "Wherever they went, they'll want the quickest way to the border. So they probably just headed for the river, and that's what we'll do."

"Okay," McBeth said. "I'll leave that part up to you. But how will we track them?"

"How did you track them?" Clint asked. "Word of mouth, right?"

"Well," McBeth said. "I had no triangle on a horseshoe to follow."

"So we'll do it the same way," Clint said. "They'll be ready to hit a stage or a bank when they get back to the U.S. We'll hear about it."

"Yes," McBeth said, "we will."

They were tying down their bedrolls when Weaver appeared, moving furtively.

"We gotta get out of town," he said.

"Was last night that bad?" McBeth asked.

"Huh? Oh, I just stayed in my room and locked the door. I don't know who's madder, Angel 'cause I wouldn't let her in, or her husband because he didn't make any money last night."

Weaver hurriedly saddled his horse and mounted up.

"Let's go! Let's go!"

"Go ahead," Clint said. "We'll catch up."

Weaver rode out.

"Does he know which way we're going?" McBeth asked.

"He has an idea."

"What about supplies?" McBeth asked.

"We'll pick some up in the first town we come to," Clint said. "Just enough to get us to the border. Once we're back in the U.S., we'll stock up."

Clint watched McBeth lead his horse outside. There was

no one around, no one to say good-bye. He hadn't really expected Jacinta, but he still looked for her.

"You want some help mounting up?" he asked.

McBeth touched his back. Clint had wrapped him the night before as tightly as he could.

"I'll do it," he said. "Might as well find out now if these stitches and wrapping will hold."

He reached up, pulled himself into the saddle, and settled down. He felt the stretch, but the stitches held. So far, so good.

"I'm okay," he said.

"Good," Clint said. He mounted Eclipse, rode up alongside of McBeth. "Let's see if we can catch up to Weaver before he gets too far ahead."

They rode past the cantina, but nobody came out to watch them leave. They passed Jacinta's building, still no one.

"Maybe we should have talked to Santee's daughter," McBeth said.

"It wouldn't have done any good," Clint said. "She doesn't know he's her father. She doesn't know him."

"That's what we were told," McBeth said, "but maybe Santee made contact."

"She's just a young girl, McBeth," Clint said. "Just a girl."

"When she washed me, she wasn't just a girl," McBeth said. "I could've had her, I think, like the mother—for money."

"But you didn't."

"No," he said. "Like you said. Too young. But maybe I should've asked her . . ."

"You knew it wouldn't do any good," Clint said. "This is what will work, James. Being in the saddle again. Being on the hunt again."

"I've been huntin' him so long," McBeth said. "Maybe your help is what I need to finally get it done."

"I hope so," Clint said. "I really hope so."

# THIRTY-FIVE

Jamie Dolan divvied up the proceeds of the bank job, tossed a bag of money at each of his three men. He got half, and the other three split the other half.

"I ain't sure I like this arrangement no more," Ed Grey said.

"Me neither," Billy Ludlow said. "We take the same amount of chances, so why do you always get half?"

They were all hunched around the campfire, so Dolan stood up and faced the other two men across the flames.

"You two want my half? Come and get it."

Grey and Ludlow stood up, their hands hovering near their guns. They felt they could take Dolan. He was no gunman. That was clear in the way he wore his gun, so that he had to cross his body with his hand to draw it. He liked the way it looked, but in a gunfight he'd be a dead man.

But the joker in the deck was Santee, and right on cue they both heard the hammer of his gun cock back.

"No guns, *amigos*," he said. "If you want to take his money, you have to do it with no guns."

Dolan drew his gun and tossed it away.

"Come on then, lads," he said. "Time to change the arrangements anyway."

"That's all we're askin' for, a change in the arrangement," Grey said.

"Just a little bigger cut, is all," Ludlow said.

"I was thinkin' more of a two-way split," Dolan said. "You boys are out."

Both men stiffened as they realized what the big Irishman was saying.

"But still," Dolan said, "I'm a fair man. If you can take my money from me, you can have it."

The men considered their options.

"What if we just wanna ride?" Grey asked.

"Not one of your options, I'm afraid," Dolan said.

"What are our options?" Ludlow asked.

"Take my money from me," Dolan said, "or die."

"Hand to hand?" Grey asked.

"Two against one?" Ludlow said.

"You drop your guns," Dolan said, "and Santee will holster his."

The two men exchanged a glance, then unbuckled their gunbelts and tossed them away.

"That's it," Dolan said, flexing his big hands. "Now come on . . ."

Santee drew his gun again.

They found a portion of the river shallow enough to cross. "Shallow" enough meant it only came up to their horse's withers. Clint kept an eye on McBeth, who had never crossed a river this deep on horseback before. The Irishman turned out to be an accomplished horseman.

When they reached the bank on the U.S. side, their pants were wet from the thigh down.

"We lose anything?" Clint asked.

They each had a burlap sack looped around their saddlehorns, filled with supplies they'd picked up a couple of days ago when they'd reached a town with a general store.

"Naw, I got everythin'," Weaver said.

"So do I."

"How you doing, McBeth?" Clint asked.

"A little winded," McBeth said. "The current was pretty strong."

"If you give your horse his head, he'll usually get you across," Clint said. "Let's step down and take a rest here."

They dismounted and Clint decided they needed some coffee, so he told Weaver to build a fire and make some. McBeth found a large, round rock and sat down on it. He'd been riding for three days now, and he'd been right about his wound. The stitches didn't pull as much today as they had the first day.

"Your bandage get wet?" Clint asked, moving over to join him.

"No, it's dry."

Clint stepped behind McBeth and took a quick look. If the stitches had separated, he wasn't bleeding through his shirt.

"It's fine," McBeth assured him. "You think they crossed here?"

"No way to tell," Clint said. "There are a lot of tracks, so lots of people have crossed here. If they didn't, then I'm sure they did somewhere along the way. I'm willing to bet they pulled some kind of job at the first likely town they came to."

"Likely?"

"Some kind of store or bank in a town without much in the way of law."

"Maybe the next town?" Weaver asked, arriving on the scene with wood for the fire.

"If not, we'll sure hear about it in the next town," Clint said.

"Why would they not have robbed a bank in Mexico?" McBeth asked.

"Several reasons," Clint said. "First, it's Santee's home, and I bet he likes to go back whenever he can, without being wanted. Also, they wouldn't want to have to deal with Mexican soldiers, or a Mexican prison. And third . . . all they'd get for their trouble would be pesos. No, they'd hold off until they got back to this side of the border, and they'd be impatient to fill their pockets with American dollars."

Weaver got the fire going, and a pot of coffee. Before long they all had a cup in their hands.

"Are we campin' here?" Weaver asked.

"No," Clint said. "We've got a few hours of daylight. We ride that long and we'll get to the town of Silverton tomorrow. They're big enough to have a newspaper and a telegraph. If they haven't suffered some kind of robbery, we'll be able to find out who has."

They finished the entire pot of coffee, then doused the fire, mounted up, and headed out to ride out those three hours before dark.

# THIRTY-SIX

Silverton was abuzz with news when Clint, Weaver, and McBeth arrived. As Clint had predicted, there had been a robbery in the area. To Clint's surprise, however, it had only taken place three days before.

They got the news when they stopped in the nearest saloon. All they had to do was listen to the talk going on around them, and then Clint asked the bartender point-blank for some information. The man reached under the bar and produced a newspaper, The *Silverton Star*.

"See fer yerself," he said.

"Thanks," Clint said.

He scanned the story. Four men had held up a bank in the nearby town of Fort Hampton and had gotten away with about forty thousand dollars. They had also killed two people, a teller and a customer.

"That's a big haul," Weaver said.

"Too big to have been planned," Clint said. "They lucked into a bank carrying that much money."

"What does that mean to you?" McBeth asked.

"Men like them," Clint said, "that's enough money to fall out over. Is Dolan a greedy man?"

"That's hard to say," McBeth said.

"You know more about this man than anyone," Clint said. "You must, you've been hunting him for so long."

"I've been hunting him as a killer," McBeth said. "He did not rob banks in Ireland. If that's somethin' he likes now, he learned it here. So if he has become a greedy man, he learned that here, too."

"Okay," Clint said, "I understand."

"How long a ride is it to Fort Hampton?" Ben Weaver asked.

"A day, if we push," Clint said. "We'll spend the night here, rest the horses, get a good meal, and start out early in the morning."

Clint saw McBeth wince, as if in pain.

"Why don't you fellows go and get us some rooms," Clint suggested. "McBeth you look like you could use some rest."

"I'm okay, but yes, some rest would be nice."

"How about a doctor?" Clint asked. "This town's got to have one."

"He'll want to remove the bullet," McBeth said. "I don't have time for that right now."

"What are you gonna do while we get rooms?" Weaver asked.

"I'm going to talk to the local law," Clint said, "see if they know anything about the robbery that wasn't in the paper."

"When do we eat?"

"When I finish with the sheriff, I'll come over. We can eat then."

"Good," Weaver said, "I'm starvin'."

As they started for the door, Clint let McBeth go first, then grabbed Weaver's arm.

"See if you can get him to lie down until I get there," he said in a low voice.

"Yeah, okay," Weaver said.

They walked out, found McBeth waiting on the board-walk.

"Try that hotel over there," Clint said, pointing. It was the nearest and looked pretty big. "I'll find the sheriff's office."

"Don't take long," Weaver said. "I'm hungry."

"Yeah, I got that," Clint said. "I'll be over in about fifteen minutes, give or take."

They parted company. Clint decided to waste some time to give McBeth a little more rest. Weaver's appetite would just have to wait.

# THIRTY-SEVEN

Sheriff Hack Yarborough didn't know much more than had been in the newspaper. "All I know is I got a telegram warning me that they may be coming this way," he told Clint.

"Not likely," Clint said.

"Why not?"

"Because we've been tracking them since Mexico," Clint said. "The one direction I don't think they'd go is back south."

"Well, that's good news to me," the sheriff said. "Can't say I want to deal with some murderin' bank robbers."

"Have you got deputies?"

The man ran a hand through his steel gray hair. His eyes looked weary.

"I've got two inexperienced men," he said. "Good help's hard to come by these days. Seems young men ain't in a hurry to become a badge toter. Not like when we were young."

"It was a different job then."

"That's right," the sheriff said. "I heard you wore a badge for a while."

"That was years ago," Clint said.

"Yeah, well, I'm thinkin' of takin' it off myself," the man said. "What's your interest anyway?"

"I'm tracking them with a couple of colleagues," Clint said.

"You huntin' bounty now?"

"Not exactly," Clint said. "One of the men I'm riding with is a lawman from Ireland. He's tracked Dolan all the way across the ocean."

"Well, I wish you luck then," the sheriff said. "Just see if you can herd them away from here."

"Like I said, I don't think they're headed this way, but I'll see what we can do to make sure. Much obliged for your time."

"No trouble," the man said, "which is what I'm expectin' from you while you're here."

"You won't get any trouble from me, Sheriff," Clint said. "We'll be out of here early tomorrow morning. All we want tonight is a meal and a bed."

"Enjoy 'em both," the sheriff said.

"We only got two rooms, so I bunked in with McBeth," Weaver said, meeting Clint in the lobby. "That's how I know he's sound asleep."

"Let's leave him then," Clint said. "He needs the sleep. We'll bring something back for him to eat."

"Suits me," Weaver said.

They stepped back outside, looked both ways, and actually followed their noses to a nearby restaurant called The Harvest. It was dinner time and many of the tables were taken. Clint and Weaver got stuck with a table in the center of the room, which made Clint uncomfortable for more than one reason, not the least of which was it made them—as strangers—the center of attention.

They each ordered a steak dinner and a cold beer with it. Weaver had been enjoying the cold brew wherever they stopped.

"Was the sheriff able to tell you anythin'?" Weaver asked.

"Only that he hoped the Dolan Gang wasn't headed this way."

"And you think they ain't?"

"No," Clint said, "that'd be coming back the way they came. They're going to keep going."

"And what're we gonna do?"

"Keep tracking them," Clint said. "Or at least keep following. This is the closest we've been. Maybe we'll find out something in Fort Hampton that will actually allow us to track them."

"And when we catch up to them?"

"Then McBeth does what he came to this country to do," Clint said. "We'll turn the others over to the law."

"You're gonna let him kill this man Dolan?"

"That's his business, Ben," Clint said. "I'm just here to help him, and you're here to help me."

"But what's he gonna do, just kill 'im? That's against the law, Clint—"

"And you're not wearing a badge anymore, Weaver," Clint said, "so upholding the law is not your job."

"Well," Weaver said, chewing on his steak, "I don't know if I'm gonna be able to stand by and watch him kill a man in cold blood."

"I really don't think that's going to be a problem, Ben."

"So you ain't gonna let him kill 'im?"

"No," Clint said, "but I think they'll pretty much be trying to kill each other, so we're not going to have to worry about cold blood."

# THIRTY-EIGHT

McBeth slept through the night and woke up ravenous. Over steak and eggs at the same restaurant he demanded, "Why'd you let me sleep?"

"You needed it," Clint told him.

"I think I could eat a damned horse this mornin'," he complained.

Clint and Weaver just had ham and eggs and watched the Irishman destroy two plates of steak and eggs. While he was eating, Clint told him what he was planning.

"We ride like hell for Fort Hampton, try to pick up the trail from there."

"That sounds good to me," McBeth said. "This is the closest I've been to the bastard in three months. The faster we move the better."

"There's one thing," Clint said.

"What's that?"

"I can move faster than the two of you," Clint said, "even if you weren't wounded."

"With that horse?" Weaver asked. "I'd say so."

"You want to go ahead of us?" McBeth asked.

"That's right," Clint said. "I'll leave a clear trail for you to follow."

Weaver and McBeth exchanged a look.

"Sounds good to me," Weaver said.

McBeth remained silent.

"You want him dead, right?" Clint asked.

"Yes."

"Does it matter to you who kills him?"

"Yes, it bloody well does," McBeth said. "I wouldn't have come all this way if it didn't."

"Okay," Clint said, "okay. I'll just locate them, then double back and find the two of you. Then we'll go and get them."

"How's that?" Weaver asked McBeth.

"It sounds better," the Irishman admitted.

"Okay, then," Clint said, standing up. "Finish eating and I'll get started."

Weaver stood up

"I'll come along, saddle the horses." He looked at McBeth. "Then come back and get you."

"Fine," McBeth said. "I'll finish up here and be ready."

"How are you feeling, McBeth?" Clint asked.

"Actually," McBeth said, "I'm feeling pretty strong."

"Good," Clint said, "because it's going to be a hard ride from here."


Clint rode hell-bent for leather to Fort Hampton. With Eclipse moving like the wind, he got there a full two hours before Weaver and McBeth could possibly make it.

He rode straight to the sheriff's office, entered like his ass was on fire.

"Whoa, whoa, friend," the lawman said. The sheriff stood up, topping six three easily, with a shock of gray hair standing up on his head, adding a few inches. There was a deputy there, who almost pulled his gun.

"Take it easy, Jed," the sheriff said, stopping the deputy with a wave of a big hand. "Friend, I'm Sheriff Bez. What's on your mind?"

"Sheriff, two colleagues and I have been tracking the Dolan Gang for months," Clint said. "We heard they robbed your bank."

"About four days ago," the sheriff said. "Killed two people."

"Have you been out looking for them?"

"I had a posse out for two days," the lawman said. "Most of them had to come back after that."

"You quit after that?"

Bez bristled.

"*Quit* ain't the word I'd use," he said gruffly.

"I'm sorry," Clint said. "I didn't mean any offense. We've just been after them for a long time."

"You and who else?"

"I'm riding with a man who followed Dolan here from Ireland."

"He must want him pretty bad."

"Real bad."

"Well, I'm pretty sure they're out of the county by now. We did manage to find a camp of theirs, but not much else."

"Can you take me to that camp?" Clint asked. "Give me some idea what direction they were heading when you . . . broke off your pursuit?"

"Sure," Bez said, "I can do that. Don't see why not."

"Now?"

"Don't you want to rest?" the lawman asked. "Looks like you rode pretty hard to get here."

"I did," Clint said, "but this is the closest we've been in three months."

"Okay," Bez said, grabbing his hat. "I'll saddle up. Jed, you hang around here. You're in charge."

"Yes, sir."

"I'll get my horse and meet you in front of the Big Thicket Saloon. You look like you could use a beer."

"I could," Clint said. "I'll meet you there."

* * *

Clint went into the Big Thicket Saloon and had a cold beer. He was standing out in front of the saloon when the sheriff rode up.

"That's an impressive horse," the lawman said.

"Got me here in no time from Silverton," Clint said proudly.

"Where are your partners?" the sheriff asked.

"They're coming," Clint said, patting Eclipse's neck. "They couldn't keep up. I want to locate the gang as soon as I can."

"Well, you're still gonna have some ridin' to do," Bez said, "but I'll take you to the campsite we found. Maybe it'll tell you somethin' it didn't tell me."

"I hope so."

# THIRTY-NINE

Clint and Sheriff Bez rode into the cold camp. While Clint dismounted, the sheriff remained in the saddle and kept a sharp eye out.

Clint walked the camp, studying the ground. He went over to where the horses had been picketed, hoping to find something distinctive in the tracks.

"Anythin'?" Sheriff Bez asked.

Clint stood with his hands on his hips, spoke while he continued to study the ground.

"I'm not finding anything about these horse's tracks, but . . ." He stopped and walked over to the cold fire.

"What is it?"

Clint held up a hand to ask the sheriff to be patient a moment. He studied the boot prints the men left behind and found what he was looking for.

"One of these fellows has worn down his left boot heel on the inside," Clint said. "Probably favors it when he walks."

"Can you use that to track a man?" Bez asked.

"Long as he gets off his horse from time to time," Clint said. "And a man's got to do that to keep his ass from getting stuck to the saddle."

"So you got somethin' you can use."

"Looks like."

Clint mounted up.

"Can you take me to where you broke off the pursuit?" he asked.

"County line," the lawman said. "Just a few miles from here."

When they reached the county line, Bez said, "My best guess is they continued to ride east."

"They keep going that way, they'll hit Louisiana," Clint said.

"If they don't turn north."

Clint looked at the big lawman. If Clint had been wearing the badge, he would have followed the gang as far as he had to, but the fact of the matter was Bez had no jurisdiction beyond this line.

"What's your first name?" Clint asked.

"Brad."

Clint put out his hand.

"Thanks for your help."

Brad Bez shook hands and said, "Wish I coulda done more."

Clint watched the man head back to Fort Hampton, then called out.

"When my friends get to town, would you tell them which way I went?"

Bez turned in his saddle.

"I'll do better than that," he promised. "I'll show 'em."

"They might even be there when you get back," Clint said. "Ben Weaver and James McBeth are their names."

"I'll remember," Bez said. "Good luck to you."

"Thanks, Sheriff."

The man turned and gigged his horse into a trot. Clint watched until he was out of sight, then turned Eclipse's head east.

"We'll camp soon, big boy," he promised. "Let's just see if we can't find something else out while we've still got some light to work with."

Eclipse bounced his big head up and down as if in assent, and off they went at a brisk walk.

# FORTY

Dolan pointed east.

"Where do we end up if we keep going that way?" he asked over breakfast.

"Louisiana."

"What is there?"

"Gumbo, women, New Orleans—"

He looked across the fire at Santee.

"Any banks?"

"A lot."

"Can we get some more men?"

"A lot."

"And that way?"

He was pointing north.

"More of Texas," Santee said. "A lot more of Texas."

"And banks?"

"Yes."

"More men?"

Oh, yes."

"One more question before I decide."

"What is it?" Santee asked.

"What is gumbo?"

\* \* \*

Clint had camped for the night, hoping that Weaver and McBeth would not try to keep riding after dark. Neither of them was particularly adept at this kind of traveling, and he was sure one of them would end up falling if they tried it. If they were smart, they'd camp and catch up to him the next day—today.

Clint had a cold breakfast of jerky and water before continuing on. He had ridden only a few miles when he spotted something a few hundred yards ahead.

"Horses," he said to Eclipse. "With saddles. Come on, big boy."

There were also buzzards circling, so he had an idea of what he would find.

There were two horses wandering about. As he approached they shied away from him, but he managed to ride one down. He grabbed the reins, dismounted, and checked the saddle and saddlebags. There was a rifle in the scabbard, but the saddlebags were empty. He turned to look for the other horse, saw it standing a few yards away, worrying something on the ground. He kept hold of the first animal and walked to the second. The animal was pushing at a dead man with its snout. There was a second man, also dead. Both bodies were lying by an extinguished campfire.

He grabbed the second horse's reins, then examined the bodies. They had both been shot in the back. The second horse's saddlebags were also empty.

"Well," Clint said, "they were shot and robbed, or they were part of the gang." He looked at the two horses. "Thieves would have taken everything, horses and saddles. So you fellows didn't get your share. Dolan and Santee got it all."

He checked the heels of both men, hoping it wasn't one of them who had the worn down left one. It wasn't.

It was getting dark and he wanted to camp, but not by the dead men, who had already been visited by various forms of wild life. The buzzards overhead were just waiting for Clint to leave.

He didn't have the time or the inclination to bury the two men. He shooed the horses away after unsaddling them, just dropped the saddles down next to the dead men.

He mounted up, stood in his stirrups, and looked behind him. Unless McBeth's wound had reopened, he figured his two colleagues would be catching up to him anytime now. He hoped to have some sort of trail for them to follow when they did.

He turned Eclipse's head east.

Riders had a habit of using the same likely spots to stop and either rest or camp. That was why Clint was able to find such a place, littered with the run-down left heel mark, which was obviously being left by either the Mexican, Santee, or the Irishman, Dolan. It showed Clint that he was on the right track, that the men had obviously decided to keep going east, to Louisiana.

Weaver and McBeth were still nowhere in sight, and they were not going to be able to catch up to Eclipse if Clint kept going. Since he'd determined that Louisiana was the outlaws' goal, he decided to turn back the way he came, hoping to join up with Weaver and McBeth before long.

McBeth remained in his saddle while Weaver stepped down to check the bodies.

"Dead," he said, mounting up again. "Shot in the back."

"Not Dolan's style," McBeth said.

"Maybe it was Santee's style," Weaver suggested.

McBeth looked at the buzzards overhead. From the looks of the bodies, they had interrupted the birds' quest for carrion.

"Clint's got to be just up ahead," Weaver said. "But we'll never catch up to him and that monster he rides unless he comes back to us."

"I suppose we should take this as a sign that we are goin' in the right direction," McBeth said, indicating the bodies.

"Well, let's leave them to the buzzards and keep goin'," Weaver said.

McBeth stretched a bit in his saddle.

"You okay?" Weaver asked.

"I'm fine."

"Stiches holdin'?"

McBeth felt behind him, didn't find any wetness.

"They seem to be."

"Good."

"They just have to hold long enough," McBeth added. "Just long enough."

# FORTY-ONE

The terrain was flat enough that Clint spotted Weaver and McBeth just as they saw him coming toward them in the distance. The two riders stopped and waited for the lone rider to reach them.

"About time you came back lookin' for us," McBeth said.

"Not my fault you're both riding donkeys," Clint said.

"Did you find them?"

"I guess you saw the bodies?" Clint asked.

"Yep," Weaver said. "Back-shot. You figure Dolan and Santee didn't want to split?"

"That's what I figure."

"Where do you think they're headed?" Weaver asked.

"East to Louisiana," Clint said.

"What's north?" McBeth asked.

"Just a whole lotta Texas," Weaver said.

"What's in Louisiana?"

"Gumbo," Clint said, "and women . . ."

"No women in Texas?" McBeth asked.

"Oh, a lot of them," Clint said, "but no gumbo."

"Dolan will want to go someplace he's never been," McBeth said, "so I'd say Louisiana."

"One of them has a run-down heel on his left boot," Clint said. "Dolan favor his left leg?"

"No," McBeth said, "at least not when he left Ireland."

"Okay, so maybe it's Santee," Clint said, "but it gives us some sign we can read."

"So there's only two of 'em now," Weaver said.

"Looks like," Clint said, "but my guess is Dolan's being advised by Santee."

"Which means?" McBeth asked.

"They're probably going to pick up some more men along the way."

"And work with them until there's another big score they don't want to split?" Weaver asked.

"Right. That Dolan's style, McBeth?"

"Not normally," McBeth said. "He kills women, not men."

"So back-shooting the other two was probably Santee's idea."

"Dolan must be acquiring new habits," McBeth said.

"Robbin' banks and killin' tellers instead of women?" Weaver asked.

"He'll revert back, though," Clint said. "A man can only change habits for so long, and then he gets the urge." He looked at McBeth. "That what you figure?"

"That's what I'm thinkin'," McBeth said. "What are the women in Louisiana like?"

"Well-mannered," Clint said, "delicate, beautiful . . ."

"Then he won't be able to resist," McBeth said.

"So we have to get to him before he can get to another woman," Weaver said.

"That's not likely," Clint said. "They're far enough ahead of us that they'll hit Louisiana before us, if they haven't already."

"Where will they end up if they keep going east?" McBeth asked.

"Probably a town called Natchitoches."

"Is that a big place?"

"There's bigger."

"Like what?"

"Well, if they head northeast and bypass Dallas they could end up in Shreveport."

"What's there?"

"Everything I already said," Clint said, "plus every vice you could imagine."

"Let's go there," McBeth said.

"Instead of followin' them?" Weaver asked.

"If Dolan is guided by Santee," McBeth said, "and he is asking the same questions I am, I believe they will go to the larger town."

"Shreveport," Clint said.

"Shreveport."

"They're three, maybe four days ahead of us," Clint said.

"They might get to Natchitoches," McBeth said, "and then go to Shreveport. We could close the gap."

"We'd be taking a chance on losing them," Clint said. "I mean, if they hit Natchitoches, they might go south to Alexandria, and then east to New Orleans."

"And what is there?"

"More than they got in Shreveport," Clint said.

"But it is farther."

"Yes. In fact, if you're right—if they go to Natchitoches and then decide to go to Shreveport, they actually have to head north and back west a bit."

"Which means?" Weaver asked.

"Which means we could beat them to Shreveport," Clint said, "if that's where they decide to go."

"All right, then," McBeth said, "Shreveport it is."

"Okay," Clint said. "It's your call."

"Just one thing," McBeth said.

"What's that?" Clint asked.

The Irishman looked at him and said, "What is gumbo?"

# FORTY-TWO

## SHREVEPORT, LOUISIANA

As soon as they arrived in Shreveport, McBeth said, "Oh yes, this is the kind of town Dolan will like."

They rode past a cathouse where the girls were out on a balcony with their tops down. They were calling out to the passing men in charming Southern accents.

"Dolan won't be able to resist," McBeth said.

Clint reined his horse in. Weaver and McBeth went a few more yards before they realized Clint had stopped, so they turned and came back.

"What is it?" McBeth asked.

Weaver looked up at the balcony, where the women were throwing kisses.

"You wanna go in?" he asked Clint.

"No," Clint said, "but if Dolan won't be able to resist, why should we go any farther?"

"You mean just watch this place?" Weaver asked. "What if Dolan and Santee don't ride down this street?"

"Good point," Clint said, "so let's talk to the local law, find out how many places there are in Shreveport like this."

"And if there's more than three?" Weaver asked.

"We'll find out which are the top three and watch those," McBeth said. "Dolan will want the best."

"What if he's changed since he came to this country?" Weaver asked. "What if he's totally changed?"

"He may have changed," McBeth said, "but it won't be totally. He's going to get the urge while he's here. I know it."

Clint figured that more than knowing it McBeth was hoping it, but either way it seemed the play to make.

"Let's find the nearest hotel, and then the law," Clint said.

They checked into a hotel, saw to the horses, and then Clint suggested he go and talk to the law.

"Why don't you two take a walk around, see what you can see. We can meet back at the hotel in an hour."

"Shreveport is a pretty big town," McBeth said. "We're not going to just run into him."

"You never know," Clint said. "Just keep your eyes and ears open."

"Sure," Weaver said.

"And while you're at it, find a doctor," Clint said. "If we end this thing here, that'll be your next step."

After asking for directions, Clint found the local law in a fairly modern building. He knew there had to be a sheriff somewhere, so he decided to go in and talk to somebody since he was already there.

He ended up talking to a young lieutenant named Burkett, who didn't seem to recognize his name.

"You want to know what?"

"How many whorehouses are in town."

"You need more than one?" the man asked.

"I need three," Clint said, "and if there are more than three, then I need to know the three best."

"Can I ask . . . why?"

"Sure," Clint said. "I'm looking for someone and he likes whores. I figure he'll go looking for one as soon as he gets to town."

The lieutenant frowned, but said, "Well, okay. We got about half a dozen cathouses, but there are also some saloons—"

"I just need the whorehouses," Clint said. "Which three are considered to have the best girls?"

"Well, there's . . ."

Clint met up with Weaver and McBeth back at the hotel, told them what he'd found out from the local police.

"They got a police department?" Weaver asked.

"Yeah, a pretty modern one," Clint said. "Might be something you could look into, Ben, when this is over."

"What about the whorehouses?" McBeth asked.

"I've got the names and address of the three that are generally considered to have the best girls—and the one we passed on the way into town is one of them."

"So what do we do, take one each?" Weaver asked.

"That's exactly what we do," Clint said. "And nobody tries to take them alone."

"Well," Weaver said, "we ain't gonna know Santee on sight."

"I will describe Dolan so either one of you will recognize him," McBeth said.

"But nobody moves without somebody to watch their back," Clint said. "If one of us sees Dolan, we follow him, find out where he's staying, and then we'll approach him together."

"I don't care what you do with Santee," McBeth said. "The two of you can take him, but Dolan is mine. I've come too far, too long, to let somebody else have him."

"That's not a problem, McBeth," Clint said. "He's all yours."

"Fine."

"Let's get a meal," Clint said, "and a good night's sleep, and we'll start watching tomorrow afternoon."

"Why not tonight?" McBeth said.

"Because we need some rest."

"I'm fine."

"Okay, then Ben and I need some rest," Clint said. "Come on, McBeth, I have the feeling this is all going to end right here in Shreveport. You can wait one more night."

"I don't know—"

"I'll buy you some gumbo," Clint said.

"I can go for that," Weaver said, "even though I ain't never had it."

"All right," McBeth said, "we'll go have some gumbo."

# FORTY-THREE

It took Jamie Dolan and Santee two days to collect three extra men while they were in Natchitoches, which is the reason they arrived in Shreveport two full days after Clint, McBeth, and Weaver.

"Let's get some hotel rooms, and then something to eat," Dolan said, "and then Santee, I want to see one of these whorehouses you were tellin' me about."

"As you wish."

They stopped at the first hotel they came to, which was not the hotel that Clint was in. And because they had killed Grey and Ludlow and stolen their share of the bank job, Dolan generously got his three new men—Edwards, Hicks, and Morris—their own rooms. They thought he was the best boss they'd ever had.

"Where do we get the best steak in town?" Dolan asked the clerk.

"Down the street, sir," the clerk said. "A place called Constantine's."

"Okay," Dolan said. He turned to his men and said, "Get settled in your rooms and meet me and Santee at that restaurant. Got it?"

"We got it, boss," Morris said.

They went upstairs to their rooms thinking, best boss they ever had.

Weaver, McBeth, and Clint had been having their meals at different times, so that they weren't off the street all at the same time. Once Weaver had found Constantine's, he decided to have all his meals there—breakfast, lunch, and dinner. So he was sitting at a table, devouring a steak, when the three men walked in and asked for a table for five. They looked like they had just come in off the trail. He kept a wary eye on them until two more men arrived to join them. A Mexican, and a big man who matched McBeth's description of Dolan to a T.

And to add to it, the Mexican was favoring one leg.

The left.

"It's a helluva coincidence, huh?" Weaver asked Clint two hours later.

Clint hated coincidences, so he said, "No, it's just . . . a lucky break. Instead of having to wait for him to go to a whorehouse, he ends up in the same restaurant with you."

"But . . . that's a coincidence."

"Let's go." Clint stood up from the table he'd taken in the café across from the whorehouse. "Let's go and collect Mr. McBeth and tell him the news."

McBeth had chosen a storefront across from the second whorehouse on their list and was sitting on a wooden chair, watching.

He started to get up when he saw Clint and Weaver approaching, but Clint waved him back into his seat.

"What are you doing here?" the Irishman asked.

"Weaver found them."

"Them? Dolan?"

"Dolan, Santee, and three others."

"Three more?"

"They must have enlisted them along the way."

"Where were they?" McBeth asked.

"They walked into the restaurant where I was eatin'," Weaver said. "And I followed them to their hotel."

"Where is it?" McBeth asked excitedly.

"Right across the street from ours. But they're not there now. They went to a saloon down the street."

"What are we waitin' for?" McBeth said, standing.

"Wait, wait," Clint said. "There are five of them, McBeth. We can't just walk up to them."

"Why not?" McBeth asked. "Maybe there are five of them, but I have the Gunsmith on my side. You and Weaver take care of the others. I'll take care of Dolan."

"And what do you want me to do?" Clint asked. "Kill them all? He's just collected these three men since he killed the other two. We don't even know if they've done anything."

"Yet," McBeth said. "You know it's only a matter of time."

"I'm not going to kill them because they might do something," Clint said.

"Fine," McBeth said, "Stay here, or go to the hotel. Weaver and I will handle it."

"What?"

"He killed my wife!" McBeth said to Weaver.

Weaver, shocked because he had not heard that before, said, "I'm really sorry about that, McBeth, but I'm not about to face five guns with only you to back me up."

McBeth glared at the two men.

"Fine," he said finally, "what do you suggest?"

"We get him away from the others," Clint said. "Either him alone, or with Santee."

"How do we do that?"

"I have an idea."

# FORTY-FOUR

Santee didn't know how he did it, but he talked Dolan out of going to a whorehouse that night.

"You smell like a horse," he said.

"Believe me, boyo," Dolan said, "the lass I pick isn't going to mind."

"This is Shreveport," Santee said. "They won't even let you in before you take a bath."

"A bath?" Dolan looked appalled. "I don't see you taking a bath."

"I don't want to go to a whorehouse," the Mexican pointed out.

"Okay," Dolan said reluctantly, "I'll take a bath . . . but in the mornin'."

"*Bueno*," Santee said. "Now have another drink."

The Mexican and the big Irishman were standing at the bar while the other three had taken a table together.

"Those three are not very smart," Santee said.

"That is exactly why I chose them," Dolan said, waving to the bartender.

Clint thought they lucked out when Dolan passed on going to a whorehouse that night. He, Santee, and his men, after a few drinks, gave in to the fatigue from riding all day and went to their rooms.

Weaver followed them from the saloon to their hotel, then crossed the street to meet with Clint and McBeth at their hotel.

"If we're gonna do this," he asked, "why don't we also do it to Dolan?"

"I'm going to take Dolan in the street, face to face," McBeth said.

Weaver looked at Clint, who just shrugged.

"What about Santee?" he asked.

"Dolan may not leave the hotel without Santee," Clint said. "Remember, he's his guide."

"Okay," Weaver said, "if that's the way you wanna do it."

"You got the room numbers?" Clint asked him.

"Yup."

"Then let's go," Clint said. "And remember, this has to be done without a shot."

Clint went down the hall to room seven. Farther along Weaver stood in front of room nine, and McBeth in front of ten. While Dolan's men had their own rooms, they did not have large rooms like he and Santee did, so those two were on a different floor.

All three men drew their guns, knocked on the door lightly with the barrel, and waited. Clint hoped that none of the men had acquired the habit of answering the door with a gun in their hand. As it happened, all three men had been awakened and stumbled to the door blearily.

The door to seven opened, a filmy eye appeared, and Clint pressed the barrel of his gun against the man's forehead.

"Back up and don't make a sound."

The man's eye widened and he did as he was told . . .

\* \* \*

Within minutes Edwards, Hicks, and Morris were trussed up on their beds—tied securely and gagged.

"Be back sometime tomorrow," Clint said to Morris. "Meanwhile, get a good night's sleep."

He stepped into the hall and, from the lack of any shooting, assumed things had gone well in rooms nine and ten. In moments both McBeth and Weaver appeared.

"Okay, we're all set," Clint said.

"I still think we should take Dolan this way, and the Mexican," Weaver said.

"If you want to sit this out tomorrow, I'll understand, Ben," McBeth said.

"I didn't say that!" Weaver snapped. "Don't worry, I'll be there."

"Okay, then," Clint said, "first light in the lobby."

They went to their own rooms, although none of the three of them expected to get any sleep.

# FORTY-FIVE

Clint was in the lobby when McBeth came down the steps, looking wide awake. On the other hand, Weaver stumbled down the stairs.

"Ben, take up a position across the street," Clint said, "in front of the hardware store. I'll be in front of the empty storefront. James . . ."

"I'm going to wait right out front," McBeth said. "I want to be right there when Dolan walks out."

"Are you any good with that hogleg, McBeth?" Weaver asked nervously.

"I could ask you the same question, Ben," McBeth said.

"I guess we're going to find out the answer to both questions," Clint said, "aren't we?"

They had to wait two hours, and then things did not go quite as planned, mostly because Santee was not a fool.

When Dolan appeared, coming out the front door, he had Santee next to him, and then coming out behind him, wearing their guns, were Edwards, Hicks, and Morris, all smirking.

"Crap," Clint said.

\* \* \*

Dolan stopped as McBeth stepped into the center of the street.

"It was a good plan, James," Dolan said. "Lucky for me, Santee doesn't sleep real well. He saw you and your friends skulking around the lobby and the halls and then checked on Morris, Hicks, and Edwards."

"This has been a long time coming, Jamie," McBeth said.

"Aye, it sure has," Dolan said. "Dublin to Shreveport. I've really liked the American West. Have you?"

"Very much," McBeth said, "and I'd like it more if you weren't in it."

"So," Dolan said, "how do we do this? I assume you want to go man to man, since you didn't try to tie me up in my room last night."

"We've always known it would be you or me, Jamie."

"Aye, but we didn't think it would come to this," Dolan said. "A Western shoot-out. Exciting, eh?"

"If you want to see it that way."

When the pedestrians realized something was going on, they got off the street, looking for cover.

Once Clint realized what was happening he stepped into the street, signaling Weaver to do the same.

"Ah, crap," Weaver said, stepping down from the boardwalk.

As Clint moved up to McBeth's right, Dolan said, "Do ye want to introduce me to yer friends, James?"

"This is Ben Weaver on my left," McBeth said. "Used to be a lawman in El Paso. And on my right is someone you may have heard of since you came to the West. This is Clint Adams."

"Clint Adams?" Dolan asked, frowning.

Santee leaned in and said something to him.

"Ah, the famous gunfighter, the Gunsmith," Dolan said. "You've done yerself proud, Jamie. Five against three doesn't seem like such a disparity in the odds now, does it?"

"Four against two, Jamie," McBeth said. "You and me, that is something separate."

"Santee?" Dolan asked. "You got any problem facing the Gunsmith?"

"I would consider it an honor," Santee said, "to be the man who kills the Gunsmith."

Clint decided to keep silent and let McBeth do all the talking.

"I'm sure Clint is not all that worried about Mr. Santee, who he had never heard of before this. But enough talk, Jamie. The talk and the huntin' is done. I'm just glad I caught up to you before you could kill any more women."

"You know," Dolan said, "I've come to like the American West so much that even after I kill you and I'm no longer on the run, I think I'll stay awhile. There are many, many women whose acquaintance I still need to make."

"No more women, Jamie," McBeth said. "Not for you."

Dolan waved to his men and said, "Step aside, gents, and take care of your own business."

But Clint could see on the faces of Morris, Hicks and Edwards that they didn't exactly think of this as "their business." Especially after they found out who he was.

"Your men don't look so sure, Dolan," Clint said.

Dolan frowned, looked at the three men he and Santee had hired in Natchitoches.

"We ain't been ridin' with you long enough to take a hand in this, Dolan," Morris said, and his partners nodded.

"You ain't payin' me enough to face the Gunsmith," Edwards said, and Hicks nodded.

"Step aside then!" Dolan growled. "I'll deal with you three later. Santee?"

"I am here, *senor*."

"Adams is yours."

"*Sí*," Santee said, "I would not have it any other way."

"Ben," Clint said, "step aside, and keep your eye on those three."

Weaver wondered how he had ended up watching three men by himself.

"Crap," he said to himself.

Santee crossed behind Dolan, like any experienced pistoleer would do, so that he was standing on the big Irishman's left, facing Clint.

"So," Dolan asked, "how does this work. Do we count?"

"Just draw!" Santee said, and his hand streaked for his gun.

The Mexican was fast. It surprised Clint how fast he was. But he dispatched him quickly, nevertheless, because he wanted to watch the two Irishmen—neither a gunman—go at it.

The bullet struck Santee in the chest, pierced his heart, and dropped him, and Clint still had time to turn and watch.

Dolan's big hand grabbed for his gun, and it seemed to get stuck in the holster. At the same time McBeth grabbed for his gun. He got it out of his holster, but it almost went flying from his hand. He double-clutched, caught it before he could lose it, and righted it just as Dolan got his loose from his leather.

They both fired twice and missed, although McBeth did take out one hotel window.

On the third shot McBeth's bullet finally struck Dolan in his huge chest. The man looked startled, fired at McBeth again and missed, and then McBeth's fourth shot took Dolan in the forehead. When he hit the boardwalk with his back, it felt like an earthquake.

It got very quiet and Ben Weaver said to the other three men, "Scat!"

McBeth walked up onto the boardwalk, bent over Dolan to make sure he was dead, then holstered his gun.

It was over.

As Clint moved up next to him, the Dublin detective said, "I don't know how you do this all the time."

"I don't do it all the time," Clint said. He had reloaded and holstered his weapon. "But I get your point. You two were awful."

"That's why I'm going back to Dublin," McBeth said. "I would never survive here."

"Well," Clint said, "why don't we find that doctor we were talking about, get that bullet out of your back, and send you back home in one piece?"

"That sounds good to me."

As Ben Weaver joined them, Clint saw some uniformed policemen rushing their way.

"But first," he said, "we'll have to deal with this."

"If you don't mind," McBeth said, "you can do the talking. I'm suddenly very, very weary."

Watch for

**THE DEAD TOWN**

330<sup>th</sup> novel in the exciting GUNSMITH series
from Jove

*Coming in June!*

## GIANT-SIZED ADVENTURE FROM
## AVENGING ANGEL LONGARM.

# BY TABOR EVANS

2006 Giant Edition:

### LONGARM AND THE
### OUTLAW EMPRESS

2007 Giant Edition:

### LONGARM AND THE
### GOLDEN EAGLE SHOOT-OUT

2008 Giant Edition:

### LONGARM AND THE
### VALLEY OF SKULLS

M240AS0808